A Girl Worth Fighting For

THE UNCONTROLLED HEROES BOOK 1

KL DONN

Praise for A Girl Worth Fighting For

I love the fact that A Girl Worth Fighting For is surprisingly light compared to other books penned by KL Donn. It shows to me that she is one I can come back to time and again and not be disappointed or bored every time.

— AYA ALMINIANA

I was not satisfied with another book I was reading so I went in search of another and came across this book, this is my first time I have read anything by KL Donn and I am happy to say it was a Great Read! I fell in love with this author Petal and Cade's story was to short. But so sweet and passionate with a little angst I couldn't put this book down! I am on the next of KL's book! Happy Reading!

— KIMY

KL Donn why did you do this to me again this week? This book hits close to home in some ways. I freakin loved it!! If you're looking of a normal nanny story this isn't it. It's so much better then that. Cade and Petal's story is so heart warming that I couldn't put it down. To have a strong woman that doesn't take anything laying down and put her with a man that knows what he wants but doesn't want to be like everyone else that falls for the nanny. It takes Petal walking away from him to realize he loves her for standing up for herself and the ways she is with his kids. That he can't live with out her.

— HELEN HANVEY

Signup for my newsletter so you never miss a release.

KL's Confessions – Newsletter

Free Books from KL Donn

What's Coming this Year

Coloring pages, other printables, & family trees.

Synopsis

From USA Today bestselling author KL Donn comes the all new Uncontrolled Heroes series where the heroes took over and decided they all get a little lovin'.

Cade Larrabee is...done. Done with love. Done with women. Done with basically any and everything that isn't his kids or his bike shop. After their mom decided she was done with family life, Cade knew where his focus should be.

In need of childcare, and someone to help around the house, Cade goes in search of a nanny. One who is as plain as Jane but can be compassionate enough to handle Mac–a boy who keeps acting out–and Lily–his sweet girl who needs a woman's touch.

Petal Davies proves to be the perfect nanny. The

perfect friend. The perfect...everything. Not only does she put up with his cranky attitude, but she gives it right back to him.

Petal shows Cade day after day, time and again that not only is she the perfect woman for him, she'd be the perfect mom to his kids, and she's mostly certainly **A Girl Worth Fighting For.**

Falling in love isn't always planned and when you least expect it, your heart decides for you. Come on over to Long Beach, California to find out who falls in love, who gets naughty on the beach and if family truly is everything.

Dedication

*For all them strong women out there – whether you think
you are or not – kick ass, take names, love hard!*

Prologue

PETAL

Twelve Years Ago

"You be strong for Momma, now, Petal." Nodding vigorously, at twelve years old, I watch my mother as she packs up her bags.

"Where are you going, Momma?" I wonder, holding on to my little sister, Calla, with all my might.

Walking over, Momma kneels beside us and cups each of our cheeks. "Calla and I have to go now, Petal. We can't stay here anymore."

Tilting my head to the side, confused, I ask, "What about me?" Calla is only four years old and doesn't understand what's happening.

"You're a big girl, Petal. You can take care of yourself." Turning back around, I watch as Momma backs her own *and then Calla's bags out the door and into the garage. Confused that they are leaving in the middle of the night, I follow behind her.*

My father isn't home from work yet, but I know he's going to be angry to find his wife and youngest daughter gone. As Momma kisses me goodbye and carries a crying Calla to the car, I wave and find myself asking, "What about me, Momma?" again, with more fear than curiosity in my tone.

I know my life is changing, and until I wake up in the morning, I'll have had no idea just how much so.

ONE

Cade

"I don't have time for this, Steph," I growl into the phone at my sort-of girlfriend. She's becoming needier and more demanding of my time. Time that is precious and not hers. If I'm truly honest with myself, I'm fucking pissed off because I should have broken things off with her weeks ago.

"But, Cade, we need some alone time." Her whine makes me cringe and grates on my nerves. At one time, Stephanie was my dream girl. Sucked dick like a champ, didn't want more than I was willing to give, and she has a to-die-for ass.

But that was months ago.

I have two kids who get one-hundred percent of me, and she doesn't like it. She's jealous, catty, and vindictive. I haven't allowed her to meet them, and she hasn't insisted. The only time she even talks about them is when she's complaining about me putting them first.

Rolling my eyes, I pinch the bridge of my nose, hoping to fend off the headache I feel trying to form. "I said no, Steph. Mac has a basketball game, and Lily has dance practice." At the same fucking time. There are times where I curse my ex, Candace, for taking off the way she did right after Lily was born, and there are times where I wish she had been a good mom. The kind they deserve.

She was never in it for the long haul though. I don't know how we lasted for as long as we did, but I can't regret any of it because I have two wonderful kids.

"You need a nanny for those rugrats." Her comment is snide, but it sparks an idea.

"Talk to you later, Steph." I hang up the phone and immediately start searching for reputable agencies. As much as I hate to admit it, she's right. I've been struggling to keep up with the kids, the house, and my bike shop. I need help.

With my parents living up in San Jose, I can't rely on them to help me out as often as before they retired a couple of years ago. At thirty years old, this isn't how I pictured my life going.

I was never sure about marriage and kids until Mac came along. Candace and I were young, in lust, and having fun. Her winding up pregnant when we were twenty-one shouldn't have happened, but I refuse to look at it as anything but a blessing.

Candace took off for Vegas when Mac was almost three. I shouldn't have allowed her back into our lives when she came crawling back, broke and hollow, two years later. Mac was so excited to have back the mom he barely remembered that I couldn't say no.

She manipulated me into believing she wanted our family. That was my second mistake. It was barely six months later that I let her back into my bed in a moment of weakness, and even though I gloved up, she fell pregnant with Lily.

At first, everything was fine. Mac was excited, and I was thrilled. My shop, Controlled Bikes, was doing good despite the odds of people telling me I would fail. I thought we were leaning toward making our relationship permanent, even though I didn't love her.

How wrong I was.

The day Lily was born, she fucking ran again. Signed the birth certificate, handed her rights to both kids over to me, and we haven't heard a word from her since.

That was over three years ago.

With the help of my best friend, Jace Cooper, and my little brother, Beckett, I'm not sure I'd have made it as far as I have. It's because of them my shop is a success.

We all do a little bit of everything, whether it's welding parts, dismantling bikes, or putting them together.

Arguably, Beckett is the genius behind the graphics. Artistic his entire life, my brother is well sought after in the motorcycle community and even with some custom autobody places. I keep him well-paid after making death threats in case he ever gets the idea to leave. Beck doesn't care about any of it though. He just wants to draw and paint.

Jace and I have been best buds since grade school. When I told him of my plans to open Controlled Bikes, he was on board without me even asking. He wanted nothing more than to be business partners. I put him to work instead. He bought into the shop three years ago so Candace couldn't try to take it from me.

Thankfully, she never tried to.

"Are those nanny sites?" Speak of the fucking devil.

"Shut the fuck up," I grumble. Jace laughs.

"Why the hell are you looking for a nanny?" He's not just my friend; he's Mac and Lily's uncle, too. They've never known him as anything else. "We've got those kids covered, bro."

"Did I hear something about a nanny?" Beck comes in from the back, paint smearing his shirt.

"I need fucking help, man. I've got too much shit going on to do everything myself." Leaning back in my chair, I see Jace has his eyes glued to the screen.

"Okay." He shrugs and walks off after clicking on something.

"Goddammit, Jace!" I shout when I see he clicked *inquire* about a girl named Petal Davies. Her picture is kind of plain. Light green eyes and dull brown hair shadow most of her facial features. However, I see she's their top requested nanny, so I leave it and wait to see what happens.

TWO

Petal

I can't believe I am so freaking late! I'm almost never late. I'm told it's a flaw, that I shouldn't be so perfect, but I can't help it. I like being on time because I hate when people waste my time.

Parking my 99' Mercedes E Class in the parking lot of Controlled Bikes, I slam the door shut behind me, hearing the seatbelt get caught between the door and the jamb and I cringe. There's going to be a nice dent there.

The car is already pretty beat up. It was a graduation and birthday gift from my dad and, even though it already had nearly a hundred thousand miles on it, I've loved it. I'll drive it until it dies.

"Damn," I hear muttered from the open garage bay door as I rush past, and I know they're talking about me and what a hot mess I am. My hair is in a huge messy bun on my head, the strap of my tank top is hanging off one shoulder, and one of my shoes is untied.

If this man hires me, it'll be a damn miracle.

"Hello, welcome to Controlled Bikes. How can I help you?" *Damn* is right. This dude is hot as hell. Tattoos up his big buff arms, crooked glasses on his handsome face, dark hair, and bright blue eyes, followed by a charming smile that nearly makes me melt.

"Oh, uh, hi." *Christ, Petal, get it together!* "I'm Petal Davies, I'm here to see Cade Larrabee?" Please, please don't be this hunk making all my girly bits sing.

He chuckles, and I cross my fingers behind my back that he's laughing at what a mess I am and not because he's about to tell me he's Cade and I don't have the job. I really need this job.

"Take a seat." He nods to a line of chairs in front of the painted window with a motorbike on it. "I'll go get him."

"Thank God," I mutter under my breath as I drop my bag to the floor and grab a bottle of water from the little fridge. As I'm twisting off the cap, I see a little blonde-haired, dark-eyed girl peak around the corner of the room the hottie with the glasses just went into.

Her eyes roam me curiously as I sit and watch her. When I see her come out of her hiding spot just a little more, I wiggle my fingers at her in a wave and smile softly. Covering her mouth, she giggles and hides again.

She has to be the daughter. I'd peg her at about three or four years old. She's got to be one of the most adorable little girls I've seen. Just from her eyes, I can tell she's not only happy and well-loved but confident in both. As she looks around the door-jamb again, she takes a bolder step out and I see she's wearing a ballerina skirt and leotards. Her feet are bare and, from the messy look of her hair, I assume she's done her lessons for the day.

Taking a sip of my water, I allow her to continue her examination until I reach into my bag and pull out a bag of fresh blueberries I'd picked up at the farmer's market this morning. Her eyes widen with delight, and I gather she likes them.

"Do you want one?" She nods her head up and down so quickly I'm almost dizzy. "Go ask," I encourage. I don't know if she has allergies, and I'd never give a child something without their parents' permission first.

I hear a squealed, "Yay!" before the girl comes running back out. "Daddy said I can. May I?" The manners of this girl!

"Help yourself." I hold the open bag out to her.

Gingerly, her tiny fingers dip in and grab a couple. She pops one into her mouth and makes a funny face. They're incredibly bitter.

"Yum." She rubs her belly, and I'm already smitten with this girl.

"I'm Petal Davies," I introduce myself.

"Petal? Like a flower petal?" She appears completely enraptured with the idea.

"Exactly like it. My daddy loves flowers."

"I'm Lily!" Her excitement makes sense now. "We have matching flower names!" I nod, enthused with her. "May I have more?" Lily points to the bag of berries.

"Yes, you may. You have such lovely manners," I observe.

She beams proudly. "Daddy says they're important."

"Daddy's girl," I hear snorted from behind me. Turning, I see a boy with matching blond hair and dark eyes. They look so much alike; he must be her brother and Cade's son.

"Am not!" Lily calls back and folds her arms over her chest in a huff.

"Whatever, squirt," he mumbles and walks away. Even though he appeared annoyed, I can see the affection for the young girl in his dark gaze.

"That's Mac. He's a bully." She pouts.

"You know, Lily, sometimes the people who care about us most don't always know how to express it. I bet he really loves you."

Tapping her chin with a finger, she ponders my words before saying, "He does read really good bedtime stories."

I don't get to respond as Glasses comes out of the office followed by the hottest, broodiest, biggest man I've ever seen in my life. I have to bite my lip to hold in my whimper. While glasses grins as he goes back behind the counter, Muscle Man glares at me until he speaks and I swear it's a damn good thing I'm sitting down.

"Ms. Davies?" I nod. "Come with me." He turns without waiting and I'm breathless.

"Come on over here, prima," Glasses calls to Lily as I walk past him. "Breathe," he mutters to me. I don't think I'll ever have a full breath in Cade Larrabee's presence.

"Close the door," he snaps as I enter his office.

I've barely got it closed before he issues his next order. "Take a seat."

My body does what he says. The few seconds of silence kill me, so I do what I normally do when I'm nervous. I ramble. "I'm so sorry I was late. Traffic was horrendous, and I—" Get interrupted.

"I don't do excuses, Ms. Davies. Be on time or don't come at all. We clear?" He levels me with another heart-stopping glare.

"Crystal," I mutter. While I might be attracted to him and could possibly be entertaining the idea of worshipping at his feet, I don't need him to be an asshole. But I'll wait until I have a better read on the man before I put him in his place.

"You're nothing like the picture on the website." He scowls as he stares at his computer.

"I asked them not to use that photo. But they refused a more accurately depicting one," I explain.

"When was this taken?"

"High school graduation." I bite my tongue.

"It says you're one of their most sought-after nannies." His gaze, the same dark color as his kids' eyes, looks me over and, while he doesn't show emotion, I can feel his judgment. "I can't see why."

And that's the last straw. Standing to my feet, I grab my bag off the floor. "Look, Mr. Larrabee, I appreciate that I was five minutes late and I do look a mess right now, but I love kids, and Lily is the absolute sweetest. I would love to know more about her and Mac; however, I won't be treated with anything less than respect. You're judging me on a moment where I chose to get here quicker rather than looking how I normally would for an interview or caring for children. You don't want excuses, that's fine. I'm not looking to be treated like I'm an imposition either." And now that I'm thoroughly angered, I grab the rest of the blueberries in my bag, walk out of the office, and see Lily sitting on the counter.

"Hey there, ballerina, you enjoy the rest of these. Maybe share some with your brother." Winking at her, I leave the building and the Larrabees behind as I unlock my car and hop in. To complete my humiliation though, the son of a bitch doesn't start.

Goddamned battery. I need to get a new one. It just hasn't been important. Slamming the keys on the seat, I pop the hood and, toward the open bay door, call out, "Hey! You got a booster pack?" Walking back to my car, I lift the hood and pull the wires off the battery to make sure they aren't corroded or dirty.

"You shouldn't walk out on an interview," is grunted behind me as a huge shadow falls over me.

"You're blocking the sunlight," I tell him instead.

"Someone call for a boost?" A younger guy, with longish hair and more tattoos than the other hunky guys, comes out with the booster pack.

"Thanks," I say as I take it from his hands. It's not easy, but I've done this by myself a few times before. Connecting it to my battery, I set it on the edge of the car and rush to run the engine.

Both kids and all three men watch me as I slowly rev the engine to gain the juice it needs to get home. Dad's going to be pissed I haven't replaced it yet.

After a few minutes, I've got enough power to make it home. Unhooking the pack, I hand it back to the guy who brought it to me with a muttered thanks.

"That was cool!" Mac says as he holds his sister's hand. I knew he loved her.

"Experience." I shrug.

As I'm about to slide back into my car, Cade says, "You need to replace that."

Fighting off my eye roll, I salute him and pull out of the parking lot with a small wave to the kids. The drive from Long Beach to Huntington Beach, where I live, is only thirty minutes, but traffic is against me today and it takes me an hour instead.

It helps me clear my head and push the lust I felt

for Cade to the side. However, the small bond I developed with Lily in such a short time cramps my heart. There was a spark with this family. Something I've never felt before.

Almost like they were my own. I've never had that before.

"Hey, sweetheart!" Dad calls from the porch of our beat-up house. We've lived here my entire life. Even after Momma left, Dad never wanted to leave. It's home.

"Hi, Daddy. How are you feeling?" I smile at the man. He's the best man I know. I'll never understand why Mom ran away with Calla. I'll never forget the heartache and pain that followed for years, especially because we were never able to learn why she left in the middle of the night with my baby sister.

"Better now." He smiles at me as I sit next to him. "He's missed you, you know." Thundering steps can be heard from the back of the house as my boy comes bursting through the door.

"No!" I laugh as I'm slimed with kisses all over my face. Roman is my two-year-old Cane Corso. He's the biggest softy in the world, once you get to know him. He treats me like I've abandoned him every time I leave home. "Dammit, Roman," I grunt as he climbs over my lap.

"What the hell is that?" The angered voice can be heard from the road. Roman immediately goes on alert.

His ears press back, and his teeth are bared as he slowly walks down the porch steps and to the chain link fence.

Cade stands there with Lily in his arms and Mac beside him. Both kids are fascinated with Roman's size. To them, he must look like a horse.

"Roman, at ease." He immediately sits and turns into the sweetheart I know and love.

THREE

Cade

Why the fuck am I here? She was late, rude, and stormed out of my office. So, why the hell did I follow her home?

"He's huge!" Lily marvels as she watches the beast Petal calls a dog, his tail wagging back and forth.

"He could eat you in one gulp," Mac teases her, and I smack the back of his head lightly. "Hey! It's not my fault it's true."

"Doesn't mean you talk to your sister like that," I scold him. He's been full of piss and vinegar lately, and I'm sick of it. He's almost nine now and is becoming too much like me.

"How can I help you, Mr. Larrabee?" Petal crosses her arms defensively, and I don't blame her. I was pretty harsh earlier for no other reason than, when I saw her interacting with Lily, my cock and heart stood up to attention.

"Can we talk?" She raises an eyebrow. I'm going to have to work this apology hard.

"Come on in." She opens the gate, and the beast stands as Mac enters and watches him with a critical eye, while Lily practically jumps from my arms and races right toward him, arms wide, and crashes into his chest.

When I go to grab her, before he can bite her, I'm shocked when he rolls over to his back, eyes closed, tongue hanging out of his mouth and tail wagging rapidly, while Lily lays her head on his chest and sighs.

I think my daughter just fell in love with a dog.

Closing the gate behind me, I don't follow Petal as she walks up the steps to her house. "He's not going to hurt her. He'd rather bite his own leg off than hurt someone he likes."

"Someone he likes," I repeat. Mac was right; this thing could eat Lil in one bite. "Come on, Lily-pad, let's go talk with Petal." Damn. Why do I like the sound of her name so much? Mac walks up to the woman no problem. Lily, however, doesn't want to leave her new best friend.

"Roman, heel," the older man on the porch calls, and the dog bounds up the steps after carefully extracting himself from my daughter's clutches, but he watches her with longing in his dark dog gaze.

"Dad, this is Cade Larrabee and his kids, Lily and Mac. This is my Dad, Wesley." Petal nods and frowns as she spins on her heels and opens the screen door. Mac and Lily follow her.

"Mr. Larrabee, I'm sorry Petal was late this morning. That was my fault. She won't tell you that though." He sighs and looks into the house where Petal is already getting the kids a drink and snack. "She won't admit what a burden I've become this past month, but things are looking brighter."

"I'm afraid I didn't give her much of a chance to say anything when she came to see me. I was put off by how different she is from the picture on the nanny website." It still bothers me.

"Oh, that." His smile disappears. "She was rightly pissed when they refused to use one of her modeling pictures that show just who she is, and instead used the one where she looks like a high school girl." He shakes his head. "She doesn't let it put people off though. She loves her job and the kids."

"Model?" That shocks me.

"Oh, yeah, from the time she was thirteen to

sixteen, she modeled for a couple of makeup companies and a couple of commercials. Some clothes, too. She grew uncomfortable when her agent was only referring her for lingerie shoots. Says the only way she'll do that is if it's a maternity one."

My eyes widen with shock and Wesley chuckles.

"She's destined to be a mom one day, and she'll be a damn good one. But she's afraid to put herself out there after what happened with her own."

Before I get a chance to ask about that, Petal is coming out to hand Wesley a glass of iced tea. "Here you go, Daddy." She also hands him a pill bottle.

"A caretaker, this one is." He grins at her, and she nods her head for me to follow her inside. I have so many damn questions and can't ask a single one with my kids around.

"What is it you wanted?" She gets right to the point as the screen door slams behind me.

"I wanted to apologize for my dismissive attitude this morning," I begin. "I was taken off guard by the difference of appearance." She doesn't say anything. I can see Lil and Mac in the kitchen coloring, and I have to agree with Wes; she's going to be one hell of a mom.

"I'm used to it." She shrugs, and that pisses me off again. She shouldn't be used to it.

"Look, your references were great. I knew the moment I watched you with Lily that you were hired, but I went about it the wrong way. Could we start again?"

As she chews on her bottom lip, I'm pulled forward, itching to reach out and touch Petal as she debates her answer. With less than a foot separating us, her fragrance reaches forward and teases my nostrils as I inhale deeply.

"All right, Mr. Larrabee, we can forget this morning because I really like your kids, but don't ever talk to me the way you did this morning, or I walk and you won't see me again." Her threat punches me right in the gut.

I don't like the idea of not seeing her again.

"You got it," I agree against my better judgment. I'm not an easy guy to get along with, and I have a feeling there will be plenty more arguments in our future. "Listen, it's Friday, so how about we get a fresh start on Monday?"

"Works for me." She smiles and Goddamn does her face light up.

"Daddy, could Petal come to the beach tomorrow?" Lily comes running up to me. The girl is terrified of the water, but she loves the sand and smell of the ocean so, nearly every weekend, we're at the beach at least one day.

"I'm sure Petal is busy." I try to let her down gently.

"She's not!" is called from the front porch. Jesus. Petal rolls her eyes at the old man.

"If you want to join us, you're welcome to," I tell her.

"Where are you going?" Her head cocks to the side curiously.

"Junipero Beach." It's walking distance to our house.

"Can I bring a picnic basket?" Lily lights up at the idea, so I nod. "Great. Any allergies?"

"None. See you around lunch."

After saying goodbye to Wesley and Roman, the kids both give Petal a huge hug before bouncing out to my truck. Passing Petal's car, I remember the trouble she had starting it this morning and debate stopping to tell her I'll pick her up. Forcing myself to keep walking, I fight every instinct beating its way to the surface to take care of her.

She's my nanny.

Not my girl.

I need to remember that.

FOUR
Petal

"What am I doing, Roman?" With his leash in one hand and the picnic basket in the other, I stand on the pathway and watch Cade with his kids.

If ever I thought my ovaries could explode from sexual desire, it'd be right now. Seeing such a big, gruff man being so kind and loving toward his kids is what every woman fantasizes about.

Shaking the depressing thoughts of my mother off, I look to Roman who is dying to get to them. But he won't until I move. He's the best-trained animal I've ever seen.

"Don't fall in love with him," I mutter to myself, but Roman whines.

As we walk through the sand, the beach isn't too busy, probably because tourist season doesn't start until next month. However, it's warm enough that there are quite a few locals out here, which means I have to maneuver around them to get to where I'm going.

"Hey there, pretty girl." One guy grips my arm until Roman snarls at him and he backs off.

"Petal!" Lily screams when she sees me. "Roman!" Her squeal hurts my ears, but my dog jumps up and down with his excitement until I let the leash go, and then he runs to her, lying down and rolling over just feet before they collide.

Lily's little giggles are contagious, and I laugh with her as Mac and Cade come walking over to us. "Hey." Cade grins as he takes the basket from my hands and passes it off to his son.

"Hi back," I murmur, barely able to take my eyes off his muscled and tattooed torso. Jesus, it should be illegal to be so damn perfect.

"You find it okay?" This awkward greeting is the weirdest moment of my life.

"Mr. Larrabee—"

"Cade."

"Cade, I've lived in the Los Angeles county area my

entire life. If I didn't know where a beach was, there'd be something wrong with me." Saying his name shouldn't feel so erotic, but my entire body quivers at the use of it.

"Yeah," he looks away before turning a disarming grin back my way, "I suppose so."

"Hey, Petal! Catch!" Mac calls, and I barely have time to jump up for the frisbee he tosses my way, just missing my head.

"Mac!" Cade scolds. "Watch the head."

The boy smirks in a way only boys can. "Sorry." He doesn't look all that sorry.

"He's not." Cade scowls at his oldest child. "But I am. He's been acting out a lot lately."

"He's eight, right?" Cade nods. "Lots of friends?" We stand on the sand with Lily lying on Roman and showing him her ballerina book as Mac throws his frisbee up and down in the air.

"I guess." Cade shrugs, but I get the feeling he's not all that sure.

"Anything in particular I should know about?" I've been dying to ask about their mom, but I can gather how Mac is feeling because, at ten, I was the same way.

"Lily has only ever had me, Jace, and Beckett as influences." He frowns. "My parents retired to San

Jose two years ago, so she's only got men around her now. None of us bring girls around the kids."

My nose wrinkles at the mention of girls. "Have they had a nanny before?" He shakes his head no. "Will you be letting Mac's school know about me, in case I have to pick him up early or something?"

"Yes, they'll know. I need a photocopy of your I.D for Mac's school and Lily's dance classes." I expected that so I brought a couple with me. "How long have you been doing this for?"

Slipping my sandals off my feet, I drop my bag on the blanket he has set out on the sand. "For about two years now. I've been with three families for varying times."

Unfolding a chair, Cade offers it to me. "Why'd you leave them?"

Easy and hard answers. "The first family I was with, I actually lived with them. Both parents had highly demanding jobs, and the kids needed more than just nine to five supervision. I was with them for nearly nine months before the mom decided she was done with work and quit. I stayed on for a month to help her adjust to her new schedule and the kids' schedules. It was definitely different, teaching someone how to mother her own kids, but she was a good mom to begin with so that made it easier."

His scowl says it all. He doesn't like that I had to teach a mom to mom. A lot of people have judged when I told them why I left. What they didn't grasp though was her desire to be the mom her kids truly deserved. I'm still in contact with them once in a while, and she's the happiest I've ever seen her and so is her family.

"The last family I was with, I had to quit because my dad had a heart attack. He needed me more than they did. They were very understanding and supportive. Even paid me an extra month to help with our own expenses because Dad's insurance doesn't cover the cost of all his new medications."

"And the second family?" Cade tilts his head, watching me and the kids at the same time it seems.

"That one was less a mutual leaving as it was a lawsuit in the making."

"What do you mean by that?" he growls out.

"The father decided I could be of more use to the family by sneaking around behind his wife's back." While my words are blunt, I don't forget what he nearly did to my career because of his selfishness.

"Are you shitting me?" He looks pissed.

"Afraid not," I mutter. I don't like talking about it if I don't have to.

"That son of a bitch." My sentiments exactly.

"It's done and over with. I'm happy now and very excited to get to know Mac and Lily." I can't hide my excitement as I watch both kids. No matter what else has happened in their past, these children are loved and that is one thing I love seeing.

FIVE

Cade

I don't know if I expected Petal to actually show up or if I thought she'd call to say she wasn't coming. I definitely didn't expect her to bring the horse she calls a dog. Despite my misgivings about the beast, I've never seen any animal be so gentle with someone as squirmy and sometimes rough as my little girl.

Lily has plopped down on him like he's a bean bag chair, and he only grunts from her weight and licks her feet. As she's telling him about her books, he watches her like he understands what she's saying.

After listening to Petal tell me about her previous employment, I can't help but wonder how I can get her to be my live-in nanny. For completely selfish reasons.

My attraction to her is already a problem that none of us can afford. Hiring someone to take care of my kids was a difficult choice, but I find I'm not regretting it like I thought I would because she puts us all at ease. Even Mac.

Until the damn kid realizes he likes her and starts acting out again. Like now, giving her the cold shoulder and being rude to Lily.

"Would you guys like a snow cone?" Petal stands and peels off her white tank top to reveal creamy skin that gets just enough attention from the sun in a white and pink polka dot bikini top. What catches my attention though, besides the tightening in my shorts, is the bright pink, purple, and blue tattoo of a calla lily climbing from her hip and up under her top.

"Wow!" Lily exclaims, finally ditching the dog. "That's really pretty." Her fingers reach out to touch Petal's skin, but she pulls back at the last minute, suddenly shy.

"You can touch it," Petal murmurs to the girl.

"It's bright," I mutter, trying to counter the annoyance I feel at myself for being so attracted to the woman who is going to be taking care of my children.

I remain silent as Mac comes over to see what all the fuss is about. Before he says anything, I can see the delight in his stormy gaze. "It's kind of girly, isn't it?"

Petal snorts. "I am a girl," she points out, and I hold back my laugh as she nails him with a 'what did you think I was' look.

My boy scowls before saying, "I'll help you." That, more than anything, shocks me.

"Let's go then. Lily, you want blueberry?" Lil giggles and nods. "What about you, Cade?" Her voice catches when she says my name, and I'm horny enough to feel my dick twitch.

"Cherry." I wink as she blushes, and they walk over to the food truck. A trail of men watches as she and Mac push each other around. I see the desire in their stares and the way they cock their bodies toward her. I'd like to toss each of them in some shark infested waters.

"Daddy?"

"Yeah, Lily-pad?"

"Can we keep her?" I turn my head toward Lily as she sighs.

"What?"

"She would the perfect mom!"

Shit.

Looks like I'm not the only one who is quickly becoming attached to Petal Davies.

"That's not how this works, sweetheart." Her bottom lip wobbles, and I want to rip Candace a new one all over again.

"But I want a mommy to love me, too. All the girls in dance have a mommy." Tears well in her eyes and, I swear to shit, I was prepared for almost anything when the doctors placed this little princess in my arms, but I've never been able to handle her tears.

"I know you do, baby." Pulling her into my lap, I cuddle her because I don't know how the fuck to tell her that she deserves the best mother in the world but hers was a shit one.

"Stop touching her!" I hear Mac yell as Roman stands, head bent low, teeth bared, eyes trained on where Mac and Petal are being hassled by three guys. "She isn't yours!" my son yells again, and I can hear the tears in his tone.

I place Lily on my chair. I don't want to bring her over into a confrontation, so I pray to all things holy this dog is as smart and well trained as Petal keeps insisting. "Lil, you stay here with Roman. Don't move."

"Okay, Daddy." She pulls her blanket to her chest as Roman lets out a vicious growl. I turn my head to see one of the men putting his hand on Petal's ass as she keeps Mac behind her.

"Roman!" The dog's head turns, and despite his lazy demeanor with Lily, I see incredible intelligence in his stare. "Stay, guard." Sitting in front of my daughter, he places a paw across her lap, holding her in place, and I know he'll do as he's told.

Striding toward the escalating situation with anger rolling through my veins, Mac sees me and smirks. If the boy knows one thing, it's that you don't fuck with what's mine and, whether she knows it or not, Petal is mine.

Just not in the way I want.

Yet.

Fuck.

Hiking a thumb behind me, the boy takes off for his sister as I approach. None of them sense me until my arm is around Petal's waist and I feel her tension.

"Can I help you gentlemen?" My words are nice, my tone is not.

"I'm fine, Cade," Petal grits through her teeth.

"Yes, you are." One dick licks his finger in a derogatory manner and, before I can do anything, Petal reacts.

"Do it again," she taunts him with her fist cupping his balls in what looks like a stranglehold. "I dare you." When he begins to say something, she twists, and he's up on his toes trying to find relief. The other two back off, hands in the air.

"Sorry," he croaks.

"Remember this feeling the next time you harass a woman," she snaps as she shoves him away. "I need bleach," Petal mutters, holding her hand away from her body like it's infected with something.

"You all right?" I don't know what the fuck else to say. Girl's a badass.

"Fine," she bites out as she walks over to a sanitizer station. "Assholes like that shouldn't be let out in public."

"Not gonna argue there." Petal is a lot more than I thought she was going to be and, as much as I wanted to kick Jace's ass for picking her, I should probably send him a stripper-gram.

"Go back to the kids." She nods to where they're watching us with rapt attention. "I'm fine here. I'll be over in a minute or two." Her smile says she's fine, but her eyes tell me she's a little rattled.

Walking back over to the kids, I whistle for the dog and point him toward his mistress. I don't like the idea of Petal on her own. The mutt has proven he can be trusted.

SIX

Petal

It's seven in the morning on Monday, and I'm sitting in the coffee shop down the street from Cade's shop debating the wisdom of continuing to work for him. After spending Saturday afternoon with him and the kids at the beach, things felt too intimate.

Roman and I left about an hour after they did because I wasn't sure how to process what I was feeling. Being a nanny, I have to be prepared for all types of relationship statuses with my clients. So far, I've only had married couples and, with the exception of the one, they were good people.

To say I was unprepared for Cade and my attraction to him is an understatement. It's not just him either. Lily and Mac are two of the best kids I've met in my life. Even with only a single parent, they're so good and sweet. Lily is dying to have a female influence in her life, and as much as I want that to be me, I know it's not going to happen. I'm here temporarily like usual.

I've never wished for something that was mine since the day my mom abandoned Dad and me, stealing Calla away in the night. No matter how much we've tried to find out what happened and where she went, Dad and I have come up with nothing. Even the police were confused.

We also found out quite harshly that Dad wasn't listed on Calla's birth certificate, so he couldn't pursue criminal charges about her either.

I always thought I grew up well-rounded and ready for whatever the world would throw at me. Landing a few modeling jobs when I was a teenager could have turned into a complete career, but I've always marched to the beat of my own drum and a lot of people preferred the yes girl. I was more likely to say no than anything else.

So, I graduated high school, took some care management courses, and became a nanny. I love kids. I love spending time with them, teaching them, seeing them grow.

Until now, I thought I would have one of my own

someday. The Larrabees make me want to run from everything I'm feeling.

I get the feeling, though, that both those kids have had enough people abandon them. I won't be another to leave them. Even if that means stifling how I feel about their dad.

"How long are you going to sit here?" a masculine voice says from behind me.

"Jesus, Jace." I scowl at the hottie with his damn hipster glasses. He'd be just cute, but then he has the crooked smile, dimples, muscles on muscles, and tattoos everywhere, so he's mega hot. Until I saw Cade, I was mega-attracted. Now, no one else does it for me.

It's only been three freaking days.

"Well?" He arches a cocky eyebrow.

"I needed coffee." I hold up my long-empty cup and shrug.

"Right." The cocky bastard rolls his eyes and pulls me up from my chair. "Your car start this morning?"

"Yes." I scowl at his back, trying to keep up with his long strides. "Why wouldn't it?"

He looks back at me, and his stare says it all. "Because you need a new battery. I'll follow you." Jace walks me to my car, waits for it to start, then jogs over to his bike a few spots away. The rumble of the engine makes me shiver.

I've always liked a man on a bike. I wonder if Cade has one, too. Likely.

Backing out of my spot, I merge into traffic, go the block and half up to Controlled Bikes, and park. The bay doors are already open, and I see Beckett, Cade's brother, hard at work sketching something out on the gas tank of a bike.

"Bring it on in!" Beckett calls, pointing to an open stall next to him.

I do as he says before getting out and asking, "Why?"

"Because you need a new fucking battery," Cade barks from a door leading into the front office. Jumping, I place a hand on my chest. I hadn't expected him to be there.

"I don't need you to do that," I tell him. I've worked for everything I've ever gotten my entire life, and I'm not about to take a handout like this.

"I'm not, Beck is. Thank him." Cade turns and walks away, leaving me to stand with my mouth hanging agape.

"You're welcome," Beckett pipes up, and I narrow a glare on him.

"Do not touch my car." I point a finger at him

and rush after Cade. "Cade!" I call his name as a tall woman walks into the office. Jace scowls while Cade ignores everyone and slams his door shut.

"Well, that was rude," the woman mutters as her gaze slides over to me. "Are you the reason he's so foul?"

"What? No." I don't even know why she would assume that.

"It's very unbecoming to chase after a man who obviously doesn't want you." She huffs and raises her nose in the air like Roman when he's catching a scent.

"I'd say it's unbecoming to be a bitch, but since you're acting like a female in heat, I'll forgive you." Striding past her shocked form and Jace's laughing one, I open Cade's door, uncaring if he wants privacy. He doesn't get to treat me like that, and I told him as much.

Seeing a sleeping Lily in the corner on a princess couch, I'm careful of the volume of my tone. "What the hell?" Planting my hands on my hips, I give him my best glare, the one that normally sends most men running when they don't listen after I've told them I'm not interested.

"What?" he snaps, sitting in his chair, grabbing some papers and ignoring me.

"The way you just spoke to me then slammed the door in my face. I told you I won't be treated like that, Cade." As soon as his name passes my lips, his dark gaze crashes into mine and I lose my breath.

"Lily had a nightmare last night. She was up most of the night," he explains, and my anger deflates.

"Is she all right?" My voice softens as I stare at the little girl, really taking in her appearance. The bags under her eyes, the way she's curled into a ball, squeezing a small teddy bear.

"She will be."

"Is Mac?" I have a feeling the boy wouldn't be pleased his sister was tormented in her dreams.

"He's angry," Cade bites out.

"Why? What was it about?" Sitting in the chair across from him, I wait for an answer.

"Her mom." I hold my breath. "I've never lied to her about the woman. She's seen pictures, weaved a fanciful dream about Candace coming back, but Lil suffers from separation anxiety. It's why she's always here with me, why I go to dance with her."

"For three years, you've been there for every moment. What's she afraid of?" I remember that fear. I wasn't nearly as young as Lily and Mac are, but the agony of not knowing if you're loved, if you did something to make that parent leave, is disturbing.

His dark gaze strays to the little girl as he tells me, "She won't say." But I get the feeling he's lying. She has said, but he doesn't know me well enough to tell me.

"Cade, this is ridiculous!" The woman from out front comes barging in. I can't even say anything because I did the same. "Is she the reason you've been putting me off?" I bite my lip from commenting as I hear Lily begin to wake in the corner.

"Watch your tone in here, Steph," Cade snaps at the woman.

"Well, is she? We had a good thing going. If you tell me you left me for this... this..."

"Beauty? Gorgeous piece of ass? Sweetheart?" I supply with a laugh. Nobody else finds me as funny.

"I was going to say, ragtag child." *Child*? I mouth at Cade and he fights off a laugh.

"Petal!" Lily's sleepy voice distracts me, and I ignore the woman altogether.

"Hey there, sunshine!" I grin when she runs into my arms, her tiny ones wrapping around my neck and squeezing tightly.

"Petal?" The woman scoffs. "You certainly look like a wilting flower," she tries to scold.

Standing, I look at Cade. "Roman has an appointment today, so Lily and I will be heading there." He nods as I turn around to Steph. "I'm a beautiful freaking flower who blooms instead of shrivels like dead leaves."

"Damn, girl. You got bite." Jace laughs as I come out of the office, pulling the door shut behind me.

"Bitterness is obviously her flavor. Does Cade have a car seat in the truck?"

"Take it, Beck's not done with yours yet." Jace hands me the keys to Cade's truck and, for a moment, I wonder if I should, but I'd rather not go back in the office and have to deal with that vile woman again. Especially now that I hear them arguing.

"Thanks. I don't have a schedule yet. What time is Mac out of school, and do you know if they know I'm picking him up?" I cock my head to the side. There was a reason I was coming in early. Everything's been blown to shit now.

He nods. "He's out at three and they do."

"I have dance tomorrow," Lily supplies. "We need cupcakes," she whispers in my ear. Jace hears her and shakes his head back and forth.

"Cupcakes we'll make then. After we take Roman to the doctor."

"Who the hell is Roman?" Jace looks insulted that I might have a man in my life.

"The best puppy ever!" Lily happily exclaims, and Jace breathes a sigh of relief which makes me wonder what the hell he's up to.

Frowning, I walk out to get my bag and tell him over my shoulder, "Tell Cade to call me when he wonders where we are."

SEVEN

Cade

I 'm fucking livid. Hanging on to my temper by a thread as Stephanie bitches about why I ended things. I hadn't meant to be so bitchy with Petal, but after a night spent consoling my daughter because she wants a mommy and doesn't understand why hers doesn't love her, I'm cranky. It didn't help that all Lily has been talking about since the beach is Petal and how she would be the perfect mom.

"This!" I slam my fist on my desk, sending my pen cup dropping to the floor and shattering. "This bullshit, right here, is why you were nothing but an easy fuck. Now, get the hell out and don't ever fucking come back, Steph, or so help me, you'll regret it."

"You can't speak to me like that!" And that's how I know I was nothing but a good lay to her either.

"I can and I did. Now, leave." I wait a beat until she huffs and stomps her foot, slamming the door on her way out so the frames on the wall rattle.

"Damn, bro, you pissed her off something fierce," Beckett, my pain in the ass, little brother points out as he walks in after her.

"Thanks, tips," I mutter, dropping into my chair.

Beck and Jace both come in and help themselves to a seat across from me, sharing a look I'm sure they think I miss. I don't. The bastards are up to something.

"What?" I snap, not in the mood for their games.

"Lil all right?" Beck asks. Their concern for my kids is always genuine because they've been there every step of the way. Half the time, they're as much their dads as I am.

"Yes." I blow out a breath. "No."

"What's going on?" Jace leans forward to rest his forearms on my desk. As big as I am, this mother-fucker is bigger.

"I thought a nanny would help with their sched-ules and give them a feminine presence in their lives that they need," I explain.

"What's the problem then? Petal seems nice."

Beck cocks his head to the side, and I can see the wheels turning in his head.

"She's the problem. This is her first day, and Lily would rather call her mom than a nanny. Even Mac would like to see her more. As cold as he can be, he warmed up to her over the weekend and was talking about her with Lil yesterday." And me? Well, it's best I don't say.

"Sooo… what's the problem?" Beck asks again and, for the first time since we were kids, I question my brother's intelligence.

"Did you not just hear what I said?"

"Yeah, the kids love her, you'd like to fuck her. What's the problem?" Blunt bastard.

"I didn't say that," I mutter.

"You're also not denying it." Jace laughs.

Fucking hell.

"Go back to work," I order them. I don't need them interfering.

"Think about it, man. She's into you, you're into her, the kids love her, she loves them." Jace shrugs. "I'd say it's a match, not employment."

Sitting back in my chair, I ponder his words. I barely know Petal. We barely know her. I don't know if she's reliable or even wants kids, let alone a man with a ready-made family. She's young. What if she wants a family of her own?

I don't even know if I want more kids, if I can risk putting them through what Candace has done to us. While I never loved the selfish bitch, I didn't hate her. I felt affection toward her and, at the time, it was enough for us.

Maybe that's where we went wrong. Neither of us tried to fall in love with the other, let alone wanted the long term. Mac happened, and we were forced into what we became. Even if we weren't in love, I don't know if I'm ready to put myself out there like that. Be vulnerable again.

EIGHT

Petal

"Petal?" Lily whispers my name quietly as we sit in the waiting room at the vet's. Roman gets his yearly vaccinations today, which is another reason I haven't been able to afford a new battery for my car.

"Yes, sweetheart?" I smile at her because she's less than thrilled about the muzzle I had to put on Roman.

"Why do they keep looking at us like that?" I scrunch my nose because, while I'm used to the stares of accusation from people because of Roman's size and breed, Lily only knows the sweet boy who likes when she lays on his chest.

"Well, Roman is a sweetheart to us, and he's such a good boy, but sometimes people are scared of him because he's so big." A pure-bred Cane Corso, I sometimes swear he's half-bear. Roman is inches bigger than the vets predicted and a good fifty pounds heavier than me. That's why his training was so important to me when I got him. I knew I'd never be able to control him unless he was well-trained. Thankfully, he's better than most.

Lily's face puckers because she doesn't like the thought of someone not liking him. "You mean like Daddy was?"

"Exactly." For three, she's very bright.

Turning to face the small waiting room, Lily places her balled fists on her hips and addresses the room at large. "Roman is my friend, and he's very nice." Some people are shocked by her directness. Others laugh and appear to be a bit more at ease. "Watch," she instructs as she faces the dog. "Roman, sit." He does. "Roman, be a puppy." I don't know what to expect with that one, but he rolls over to his back, legs up in the air, and whines at Lily until she lays down on his chest like she did the first day.

One woman, who was eyeing him up pretty harshly, stands with her bright orange cat in her lap and comes to sit beside us. "It's not often we see such large animals so well-trained."

"I agree." I'm really not sure what else to say to

her. She was judging my dog pretty harshly. Interested in her cat, Roman's head picks up and he sniffs the air. His tail wags harder, making a loud thumping sound against the floor.

"Is he a pit bull?" A tremor of fear works through her tone.

"Roman is a Cane Corso, an abnormally large one actually. But he's certified trained by the American Kennel Association, and he went through some rigorous police training as well. You won't find a better-behaved civilian dog if you try." I beam with pride as Roman tries to lick Lily through his muzzle.

"May I pet him?" she asks.

"Sure." I'm happy to ease people's fears. "Roman, say hello." Lily stands, and he follows, offering his paw to the woman.

"Oh my! How polite." Her grin is genuine now as he invades her cats' space. The feline watches him with a disinterested stare until he backs off.

"Roman!" the vet tech calls, and he stands tall, waiting for Lily and me to gather our bags. "Well, hello there, miss." The tech smiles at Lily who clutches Roman's collar and my hand like a lifeline.

"You won't hurt him, will you?" she whispers to the tech. I choke up at the worry in her tone.

"Not at all. He might feel a little pinch," the tech

leads us to a patient room, "but the medicine makes sure he doesn't get sick in the future, so I'm sure your mom will agree, it's worth it." I'm stunned at the assumption.

Lily beams proudly.

Before I can correct her, Roman's vet walks in the room and talks Lily through the procedure, encouraging her to pet his back to keep him distracted. We're done in minutes, and the vet is handing Lily a treat for Roman to munch on while I pay the bill.

Once we're back in Cade's truck, I still haven't found my voice, and Lily is so occupied with taking off Roman's muzzle and chattering away to him she doesn't notice. I'm reeling as we drive, but to where I'm not sure.

Until we arrive at Cade's shop. I didn't mean to come here. It's not even lunchtime yet. We have hours before I have to pick up Mac, and I was going to take Roman home before Lily and I went to a craft store.

My mind is obviously stuck on what the vet tech said. How much it resonated in me. I'm not her mom. I should have spoken up, said something. But I didn't, and I need to know why.

"Why are we at Daddy's shop?" Lily perks up from the back.

"Oh, uh..." I see my car. "To get my car. I'd hate to get more dog hair in your dad's truck than we have to." I pray it's ready to go.

Parking his truck, I get out and help Lily out of her seat, letting Roman jump down after her. "Car." I point toward my car, and he jogs right over, sitting beside the back door.

Lily runs into the building and straight to her dad's office. Not giving it another thought, I don't see Jace up front, so I go to the door that leads into the shop to see if I can find someone.

"Petal!" is screamed from the room Lily disappeared into, and I run toward her, uncaring about my surroundings.

Entering the room, what I see is not what I expect.

There are photos of Cade and the woman from this morning hung all over the walls like a collage. The provocative manner in which they've been captured is what has the girl horrified and me feeling sick to my stomach.

"Eyes closed," I say and pick her up. Pushing my own feelings to the back of my mind, I try to ease Lily's panic. For a little girl, they must be terrifying. Her father nude, doing some very sexual things with a woman, is not something she should ever be exposed to and, honestly, I'm shocked they were up.

"Sit here for a minute." I place her in the chairs where we first met just a few days ago. Rushing to the front door, I pull it open and whistle for Roman. "Guard," I command and he sits nicely with Lily while I make sure there's no one else in the front office. Closing Cade's door, I go back to the main door and lock it so no one else can enter the building.

"I'll be right back." Lily nods, hiding between Roman's legs as he sits dutifully. Taking a deep breath, I burst through the shop door and close it behind me, appearing calmer than I feel, and shout, "Cade Larrabee!" as loud as I can.

Cade and Jace pop their heads up from the back of the shop, matching confused looks on their faces. "Why are you yelling?" Cade asks, getting to his feet.

"Why?" It's rhetorical. "Have you been in your office lately?" I'm not sure why I'm so angry about what I saw. He isn't my man.

"No, why?" Striding toward me, he wipes his hands on a dirty towel and, for some asinine reason, his filthy hands play through my mind as he works my body into a frenzy. "Petal?" He's standing directly in front of me, and I have to shake off my fantasies.

"Pictures," I croak. "Everywhere." I glare at him, remembering Lily's cry. "Lily saw them, Cade."

His concern grows as he rushes through the door and straight to his office. The amount of cursing that follows tells me this is not a welcome sight, and I feel a tad better about it.

"Lily-pad?" Cade calls for his daughter as he comes back out to see her hidden in Roman's body. "Come here, sweetheart." He tries to coax her out, but Lily burrows further into my dog.

My heart cracks at the fear she shows for a man she loves so much. She may not understand what the pictures mean, but she knows she shouldn't have seen them.

"Petal!" Lily hiccups and cries for me. The devastation on Cade's face makes me want to weep.

"I'm going to fucking kill her," he mutters under his breath and goes back into the garage.

NINE

Cade

I'm not sure what pisses me off more. The fact Stephanie invaded my space, or that Petal is now looking at me differently.

The fact my daughter saw something so erotic, something no three-year-old should ever see, angers me beyond comprehension. If Lil hadn't seen the pictures, I'd deal with Steph on my own, but she did and, for that alone, Steph will pay.

"Mr. Larrabee, are you sure of who it was?" the officer asks again. They've bagged and cataloged all the photographs, dusted for prints, and have taken the surveillance camera that showed Lily going into my office about five minutes after Stephanie left and Petal running in there less than thirty seconds later as Lily called for her.

It also shows the moment when my daughter turned her back on me, asking instead for Petal because she doesn't understand what she saw.

"Yeah, I'm positive it was her." Stephanie McCleod isn't just any woman. She's the niece of LA County's deputy DA. She's notorious for getting into trouble and having her father enlist her uncle's help to get her out of it.

"And you want to press charges?" I understand his reluctance. Every time she's in trouble and the police follow through with charges, someone gets hell. He doesn't want to be that someone.

"If my daughter hadn't seen, I wouldn't care," I explain. I need them to understand why this is so pressing. Aside from the fact Stephanie came back after I told her to fuck off.

"I understand, sir. Someone will be in touch soon." I nod as he leaves, and I'm left alone in my office to clean up the fingerprint dust.

I sent Jace with Petal and Lily to get Mac from school after they gave brief statements. I know the charges against Steph will stick because I have cameras in every area of this building, and my directive to her was very clear this morning. She trespassed. Plus, my father may be retired, but he was one of the best prosecutors the Major Crimes squad in the LAPD ever had. They won't let him down should I need to call in the favor.

"How are you gonna fix this?" Beckett asks, walking into the office.

"Fix what?" I didn't do anything wrong.

"You don't know, do you?"

"Know what? Jesus, Beck, I'm not in the fucking mood for your damn games," I snap at him.

"You and Petal, man. You're it for each other. Two minutes in the same room with you two and anyone can see it."

"No, we're not," I deny. But I feel some of what he means, which is fucking ridiculous. We don't know each other.

"Yeah, man, you are. You're too afraid of getting hurt, and I bet she is, too. But even those kids know it." As he walks away shaking his head, I try to push his words off.

But they feel right.

Like what he says is true.

TEN

Petal

After escorting Lily and me to pick up Mac, I convinced Jace to go do whatever it is he does, and we drove out to my house to drop Roman off with Dad and so I could check on him. Today was his first day back to work in a month, and I've been worried sick.

As a mortgage loan officer, his hours are pretty standard, and his job isn't as stressful as it could be. Doesn't mean I worry any less though.

"Hey, there's trouble." He laughs as I guide the kids into the yard. Roman runs around looking for squirrels to chase, and Lily runs up the porch steps to curl up on the extra chair beside Dad.

"Hi, Daddy." I smile at him as Mac goes inside looking for a drink. I didn't tell him what happened or why his sister was so upset because I didn't think it was my place, but he's a smart boy and has figured out something happened. "I'll be right back. Just gonna get her a drink and snack." With one last look at the broken girl on my porch, I head inside, my heart heavy.

"What's the matter, miss?" I hear Dad ask her. If she answers I don't hear it.

"She'll be okay, you know," Mac tries to reassure.

"I'm sure she will. You guys take good care of her." I grin for his benefit, but I don't feel it.

"Were you really a model?" It's been mentioned a time or two now.

"I was. Mostly for clothes and makeup." Pouring a glass of milk, I grab a bowl for some fruit.

"Why'd you quit?" The question was inevitable.

"I had a manager that wanted me to do things I wasn't comfortable with."

Mac is silent so I hope he's dropped it. I was wrong. "Like what?"

Turning to face the boy, I rest my hip against the counter and cross my arms. "Underwear, sometimes things so skimpy I wouldn't even wear on my own."

"Oh."

"Plus, I was sixteen, and my dad wouldn't sign off on it."

"Nobody bullied you into doing it?" Now, he has my full attention. I find, with kids, there's almost always a reason behind these inquisitive questions.

"They tried to. They offered more money, fame, popularity. All I wanted was to help Dad with the bills after my mom left."

Mac's eyes widen to the size of saucers. "Your mom left, too?"

I nod. "She did, when I was ten." I swallow past the pain. "She took my baby sister with her. I haven't seen Calla since I was ten and she was four. If she remembers me, I'll be surprised."

"My mom left, too. Twice." I ache for him.

"I'm so sorry, Mac." I can't imagine losing my mom twice.

He shrugs. "She didn't love us enough."

"I'm sure that's not true." How could someone not love these kids? "Sometimes, people aren't ready for what they have. They don't see how truly special what they're leaving behind is."

"She didn't even stay long enough to meet Lily." My heart breaks. The first time I met Lily, I knew she was dying for female influence and approval. "Are you going to leave us, too, Petal?" His bottom lip quivers and his eyes fill with tears. I can see him trying so hard to hold them back, to be strong.

"Oh, Mac." I pull him into my embrace, never wanting to let the fragile boy go. "I have no plans to leave but, ultimately, that's up to you and your sister, and your dad." There isn't a thing in this world that could drag me away from these kids.

"Why my dad?" He pulls back from my hold to wipe his eyes.

"Well, he has to see that I'm taking care of you guys as much as you need. He has to be able to trust that I have your best interests at heart."

"But you do."

"I do," I agree. "But since this is my first day with you guys, trust takes time. I have to earn his." I smile to soften the words.

"Okay."

"I'm just going to take this out to your sister. Once she's done, we'll head home and start dinner." He nods as I stand with the snack for Lily in my hands. What I hear once I get outside has me conflicted in so many ways.

"I wish Petal could be my mommy." Lily's soft voice is full of desire.

"Why's that?" I hear Dad ask her.

"She likes me, I think. My real mom doesn't." That woman really did a number on these kids. I'd like to kick her damn ass. "Uncle Jace and Uncle

Beck said Petal is perfect for Daddy, too." I hear the pleasure in her tone and decide it's time to make my presence known.

"Here you go, Lily, milk and fruit. Once you're done, we're going to head out." Taking the dishes with a soft thank you, Lily sits on the top step to eat quietly.

"Got your hands full," Dad observes as I sit beside him.

"Yeah, I do."

"It wouldn't be so bad, you know."

"What wouldn't?" My brows draw together with my confusion.

Dad levels me with a duh stare. "Being their mom. Raising someone else's children as your own. I'm sure Cade wouldn't mind either."

"I don't know what you're talking about." I try to brush him off because, the more time I spend with these kids, the more I love them and wish this would end in a fairy tale where I get the guy and the kids. But Cade can hardly stand me.

"I saw how he watched you. A man knows from the moment he meets a woman whether she's right for him or not, and Cade knows. He just won't admit he knows yet."

"Did you know with Mom?" We don't talk about her often, only when it's important.

"No. I knew she was going to be important, in giving me you and Calla, but she was never meant to be my forever. Not like you and Cade." Why is everyone suddenly pushing this?

It's a question I'm going to be asking myself a lot over the next few weeks, I think.

ELEVEN
Petal

I've spent the last three weeks avoiding Cade at all costs. I see him, of course, when I pick Lily up at his shop, and when he comes home from work. I always make sure that dinner is on the table so I don't have to stay, but I'm pretty sure he's catching on now.

Lily and Mac invite me to stay nearly every night. Lucky for me, I have the perfect excuse to leave: Dad and Roman. Although neither of them really needs me very much, so it's lame, but it's all I've got.

Cade has been pushing for me to stick around in the mornings before Lily and I leave to either go to her dance classes or a fun tot group I found. She's made so many new friends and, it seems to me, has really come out of her shell.

Jace still whispers in my ear about Cade and me, and so does my Dad actually. I'm tempted to hit them both. Possibly with my car. Even Beckett has gotten on the bandwagon.

They're breaking my heart down, or rather, Cade is. He touches me a lot, making my heart stop in my chest each time. Mostly, they're accidental brushes, but I'm beginning to think they're on purpose, too.

I want so much to allow my feelings the freedom to grow, but I've overheard enough of his conversations to know Cade isn't looking for a woman. Or a mother for his children. The last thing I want is for him to believe I want to replace the mother who doesn't deserve his babies.

"Petal?" Lily's voice calls as she claps her hands in front of my face.

"Sorry, what did you say?" I shake my head to lose my train of thought.

"Can you fix my braid? Miss Griffin doesn't do it very well." The last sentence is whispered quietly to me, but she's right. Her dance instructor isn't the best at it. Quickly, I have a line of girls asking me to fix their braids into fishtails just like Lily's.

With each finished girl, and every passing moment, they all tell Lily she has the best mom. Rather than it dimming her light, the sweet girl beams with pride and doesn't correct a single one of them. I try to, but they're gone before I can explain.

I'm sure, on some level, they know I'm not her mom because it was always her dad or uncles doing this job. But I love how innocent they are and just want to compliment her so, once again, I find myself letting it go.

"Daddy!" I hear Lily squeal and turn around to see Cade coming backstage with a small bouquet of Lilies.

"Hey, Lily-pad, I'm sorry I wasn't here to help you get ready." Handing them to her, he leans down to kiss the girl on the head.

"That's okay, Daddy, Petal makes the best braids!" She twirls around to show off the one I whipped up really quick. Cade frowns before he smooths out his features.

"Looks great, kiddo." His grin is forced as Lily is called away. "We need to talk when this is over." His curt tone and attitude don't bode well.

I nod and follow him out to the audience where Lily's class is going to be performing their version of Cats. I've been watching them practice for weeks and, for their age, it's going to be adorable.

As I sit next to Cade, there are three of the

mothers in front of us, and I know immediately they're talking about me.

"Can you believe her? Coming in with those tattoos peeking from under her clothes and that wild hair. She should be banned," one mom says, and I self-consciously run my fingers through my hair to tame the wild locks.

"The girls kept saying how great Lily's mom was, but she's not the girl's mother. I don't know why she doesn't correct them." I pale and can feel the glare Cade sends my way. If the floor could swallow me up right now, that'd be great.

As the music plays and the curtains draw back, I try my best to ignore their snide comments and Cade's obvious anger, but I feel sick about it all. I've never been sure how to tell Lily that letting people believe I'm her mom isn't appropriate. I know I should have, but breaking that girl's heart isn't high on my to-do list.

I'm in a hell of my own making as we watch the children dance and twirl their hearts out. Cade's arms are crossed the entire time and, when it's time to applaud everyone's efforts, I rise to my feet without thought.

People filter out and, when I go to step away, Cade grips my bicep so tightly I flinch. I see Jace and

Beckett coming toward us and, from the looks on their faces, they know I'm about to pay hell.

The auditorium has cleared out, and I'm suddenly alone with these men. I don't fear them, but I know I'm about to get shit.

"Got something you'd like to say, Miss Davies?" Cade grits between clenched teeth.

Guess our friendship is out the window. "No." I wrench my arm out of his grip and face him fully. I understand his anger, but I won't apologize or explain when he's so angry with me.

"Nothing? You're not going to tell me why you've been parading my children around claiming they're yours?" A storm is brewing in his gaze. Maybe I don't understand his anger.

"First of all, I haven't. Not once have I made that claim."

"You also haven't dissuaded the notion," Beckett interrupts. That's mostly true.

I take a deep breath because I don't want to say something I'll regret. I'm obviously taking too long for Cade's liking because he barks at me, "Is that why you're a nanny? To claim other people's kids and make them forget their real parents?"

Ouch. Not once have I tried to do that. "I would never do that," I tell him. My own anger is spiking and, lucky for me when I get mad, I also get emotional. "I've only ever done the job you asked me to do."

"I didn't ask you to make my children yours!" he shouts, and the few people still lingering glance over. I can feel their judgment.

"Whoa, man," Jace mumbles beside Cade. "She's great with them."

"She's not their mother," Cade snaps at his friend.

Arrow right through my heart. "You're right, Cade, I'm not their mother. I would never try to replace the woman who gave them life. I've only ever tried to be their friend, to give them happiness for the few hours in a day that I'm with them. Falling in love with them was easy. You've done a wonderful job raising them into great children." I swallow the lump lodged in my throat as Beckett curses behind me and Jace shakes his head. They obviously know what I'm about to do. "I'll bring Lily's extra car seat and her things from my car by tomorrow. Please tell her I'm sorry I couldn't stay."

Rushing away from the man I've slowly been falling in love with, and the other two I was beginning to feel a comradery with, I rush out to my car. Slamming the door shut behind me, I don't waste time driving away and merging onto the Pacific Coast Highway with no destination in mind.

My heart is shattering for so many reasons. The loss of Lily and Mac. The loss of Cade. The loss of feeling like I finally belonged somewhere and now I'm left out in the cold, a nobody.

Unloved and pushed to the side, I'm the one to leave this time.

TWELVE
Cade

"You dumb son of a bitch," Jace curses at me as he storms away.

"That was cold, man, even for you," Beckett mutters. The man who had my back five minutes ago is turning his on me.

What the hell did I just do?

"Daddy!" I hear my sweet girl's voice as she comes running for me. "Where's Petal? We were gonna get ice cream." As I catch her in my arms, she looks around for the woman she wishes were her mother.

"She had an emergency and had to leave. She asked me to tell you how great you did though." I grin and hope she catches up with me.

"Will she be back?" All Lily talks about is Petal

and the fun things they do together. Shell collecting on the beach, baking, crafts. Lily worships her, and I don't doubt for a second that the feeling isn't mutual.

So, why the fuck did you run her off?

Christ, what did I do?

Picking Lily up, I collect her bag and see a present inside of it. "What's this?" I ask Lily.

"That's for you. We went shopping!" Her enthusiasm is interrupted by a huge yawn.

"Let's go get your brother from school then we'll stop for ice cream." She grins and, for now, Petal is forgotten. Tomorrow, I know there will be questions I'm not looking forward to.

Parking in front of Mac's school, I see him frowning as he walks closer to the truck before hopping in the back seat. "Where's Petal?" Christ. I'm surely going to hell for doing this to them.

"Emergency. Get in, we're going for ice cream." And whatever else I can find to bribe them with.

Lily chatters about her recital the entire way to the ice cream shop by our house. Mac listens with half an ear as he watches me closely. The boy is too much like me. He knows when something's up and he knows now.

After ice cream, we head home and decide on

pizza for dinner. Both kids are out cold early, and I'm left to ponder how to win Petal back over.

No. Not just over. To win her.

Opening the gift Lily brought home, I admire the thick leather-bound bracelet—soft, supple, strong—with Lily and Mac's names burned into the material.

Christ, I have to get her back.

I think I was so angry because she was doing exactly what I wanted, only it wasn't because I had made the decision. Hell, if I'm really honest with myself, I didn't even care that I heard so many girls telling Lily what a great mom she has because Petal is exactly the kind of mom my kids deserve.

She's the kind of woman I've always wanted for myself. Larger than life, honest, down to earth, and she loves the fuck out of my kids.

What pushed my buttons is that she's been brushing me off for weeks. And I've let her because I wasn't sure she would ever cross that line of dating her employer. Now, facing the possibility of her not being in our lives, I'm not giving her a choice.

After a sleepless night, trying to figure out how to apologize, how to be the man she needs, I realize, I have kids. And at the moment, the way to her heart could be them.

As I'm placing bowls of cereal in front of them, I

know I need to get them on board as well. "I have a serious question for you both." Lily smiles happily, still on a high after her show. Mac watches me critically. "How would you feel about me and Petal together?"

Lily's nose scrunches as she thinks. "Like boyfriend and girlfriend?" She's too damn smart.

"I was thinking like husband and wife." I'm watching Mac, looking for any cues that he isn't on board.

"So, she would be my mommy?"

"She could be. If that's what you both wanted." I won't get her hopes up too high.

"Yes!" Lily jumps up from her chair and starts dancing.

"Mac?" I gaze at my son, my near twin when I was his age, and wonder where his head is at.

"Her mom left her, too." His words shock me. I didn't know that. "She knows what it feels like." He's going somewhere with this, so I remain silent as he gets there. "I like Petal a lot, Dad."

"Good. So do I."

"You can't make her leave." His perceptive stare bores a hole through me.

"I won't."

"You have to love her and let her love you." Jesus, whose fucking side is he on?

"I will." He nods and goes back to eating his breakfast, and I guess I have my answers. Now, to figure out how the hell to win her back after my cold accusations and general assholishness yesterday.

THIRTEEN

Petal

I cried far more than should have been possible for someone who claims she isn't in love. I keep telling myself and my dad that I'm not. But as I get ready to drop off Lily's car seat, I realize I am.

I love Cade. I love his kids. I love his damn brother and friend, too.

And now, I have none of it because I couldn't correct a few three and four-year-old girls.

Banging my head on my steering wheel in the driveway, I'm distracted as the phone rings and don't check it as I answer with a mumbled, "Hello?"

"Miss Davies?" a woman's voice says.

"Yes, this is Petal Davies." My heart races. The last time I got a call like this was when my dad had a heart attack.

"This is Principal Elaine Louise from Macintyre Larrabee's school." I sit up straighter. My number was given in case they couldn't reach Cade.

"Is Mac all right?" If they're calling, nothing good has happened.

"He's fine. In a touch of trouble, and I can't reach his father. Is there any way you can come to the school?"

"Yes, of course. I'll be there in twenty minutes." Hopefully.

"See you then." She hangs up, and I hope rush hour traffic is over. I try calling Cade three times on the way with no answer, so I finally give up and focus on the cars around me and getting there in one piece.

A near-miss accident, speeding, and rushing through a yellow light, and I make to Mac's school with minutes to spare. Putting the car in park, I call Cade one final time and leave a voicemail. "Cade, it's Petal. Mac's school called when they couldn't reach you. They said he's fine, and I'm just walking in now. Call me back, or I'll call you when I'm leaving, what-ever works. Bye."

Shoving the phone in my pocket, I pull the hem of my shorts down. I wasn't prepared to come to school, but once she said Mac needed someone, nothing else mattered. My cut-off jean shorts, with more frayed material than sewn, and my crop top tank, matched with high top Converse shoes, are not likely to make a good first impression.

As I enter the office, I see Mac sitting on a bench against the far wall, head down, feet dangling, and his backpack beside him. Relief hits me as I see he's actually all right.

"Mac?" I call his name as I walk closer, and when his head lifts, I falter. Not only is he not fine; I'm certain he needs a doctor. "What happened?" His left eye is completely swollen shut, and there's a cut on his eyebrow. Worry, quickly followed by anger, rushes through me. I specifically asked if he was okay.

"Craig Gilbert was being a jerk," Mac mumbles.

"Miss Davies?" I hear a woman's voice from behind me.

"Yes." I stand and once again dread how I'm about to meet this woman as I turn around.

"Well." Her eyes roam up and down my body, dissecting every inch of exposed flesh, criticizing the tattoos she sees. "Macintyre is in quite a bit of trouble for assaulting another student," she says, her nose up in the air.

"What happened?" I ask again.

"Let's go in my office to discuss this with the Gilberts." Great. More people to judge. I don't actually care about their opinions, but Mac and Cade might.

"Sure, Mac, you sit tight here." Grasping my cell, I hand it to him. "Your dad should be calling. Make sure you answer it, okay?" He nods as I follow the principal.

"Mr. & Mrs. Gilbert, this is Petal Davies, Macintyre's alternate caregiver." Alternate? That sounds... cold.

"Hi." I nod at them, ignoring their stares.

"Well, it's no wonder how he acts now." Again, with the judgment.

"Can someone please explain to me what has happened?" I'm beginning to lose my patience.

"Your ward hit our son." Mrs. Gilbert crosses her arms as her husband ignores everyone in the room, typing on his phone.

"Why?" I know Mac. He doesn't have a temper or a mean bone in his body.

"He claims Craig was calling him a bastard orphan," Principal Louise explains.

"I see. And Craig, is he all right? Anything broken? Stitches? Concussion?" I need more information before I can react.

"He's got a bruise on his cheek, but he's icing it so it should be fine soon." I blink rapidly at the principal's response.

"So, Mac punched him?" They shake their heads. "What did he do then?"

"The teacher says Macintyre pushed Craig, and he tripped, hitting his cheek on a desk." So, he hurt himself.

"Okay, so let me get this straight. Mac is called a bastard, and he pushes a child who then winds up tripping and bruising his cheek a bit?" Nods all around. "But then Mac is the one with a cut in his eyebrow and a completely swollen-shut eye. What happened to Mac?" If this other kid is admittedly fine, I no longer care about the whats or whys and only the how of what happened to Mac.

"Craig got back up and hit him with a textbook. We suspect the corner of it got his eye," the principal explains.

"What kind of textbook? A damn dictionary? You give this boy an ice pack for a reddened cheek, and Mac gets squat for blood and swelling? Are you freaking kidding me!" By the time I'm finished, I'm worked up and my voice is raised.

"Now, listen, he shouldn't have hurt my son," the woman tries to defend.

"No, lady, your son shouldn't be saying such nasty words to a freaking eight-year-old. Like, seriously, are you kidding me here? Mac was in the wrong for pushing him, but in what way is the treatment Mac has gotten fair in comparison?" My blood is boiling, and I have to cross my arms, gripping my biceps with painful force to stop from slapping sense into these people.

"Listen here, young lady," the father finally speaks. "Obviously, the problem is your boy. His own father couldn't be bothered to show up and take care of this. He had to send the help." The help?

"Shut up, you idiot. How dumb are you? I'll be taking Mac to a doctor, and I promise you all, if there's one stitch, one popped blood vessel in his eye, one wrong thing with him because you couldn't be bothered to attend to him properly, you'll be hearing from a lawyer." I ignore their protests as I storm out, slamming the door shut behind me. I halt as I see Cade sitting next to Mac, both with shocked expressions.

"Heard that, huh?" Mac grins so hard he winces.

Cade nods his head and stands, walking over to me. I'm rendered speechless as he pulls me into his embrace and lowers his head. He pauses for a moment, giving me a chance to pull away, but I push up, meeting his lips for a scalding kiss that makes my toes curl.

FOURTEEN
Cade

After forgetting my phone in my office while I was working on a custom bike we were hired to do, I was shocked at all the missed calls and voicemails. When I got to Petal's last one, I knew I had to get to the school myself.

Upon arriving, I was ready to go ballistic when I saw Mac. My son was bruised, swollen, and had blood on his shirt. I was livid.

Until I heard Petal lace into whoever was in that office with her multiple times. She didn't excuse Mac's behavior but focused on the lack of action taken by the school to attend to my son's wounds. I think I fell in love with her right then.

When she came storming out of the office and saw us, she paled at first, but her spine straightened, and I knew I was definitely in love with her. Now, as our tongues tangle, and her body melts into mine, I know she's mine.

"Uh, Dad?" Mac's voice is full of humor.

Pulling back from Petal, I regret the past few weeks in such a way that I should have done this the moment I met her. Brushing her wild maroon hair back from her face, I grasp her jaw with one hand. "We'll finish this tonight." I lean down to kiss her again, ignoring the throats clearing behind her and my son's laughter.

"Mr. Larrabee," Elaine's stern voice grates on my nerves.

I don't mince words as I guide Petal with a hand on her back to wait with Mac. "Elaine, from what I hear, you allowed a boy to call my son a very derogatory name and denied him medical attention when he obviously needs it. Petal said everything I would have in a much nicer manner. If there is one thing wrong with my son's vision or anything else, a lawyer will be in touch with you."

"Now, wait. That boy pushed mine first." The couple watching Petal with dirty glares fights back.

"And the shit deserved it. If he had more than a bruised ego, I'd feel bad for him. However, he isn't about to go get stitches and maybe a CT scan. Brain injuries are fickle and expensive. You can expect a call from my lawyer." Turning my back on their open mouths, I grab Mac's bag and motion for him and Petal to start walking.

"I didn't mean to hurt him, Dad," Mac says before we reach my truck.

Tossing his bag in the back seat, I kneel down to his level. "I know you didn't, son, and while I understand your frustration and hurt, violence isn't the answer."

"I know." His head hangs, and I feel for the kid. None of this is his fault, not really. "Were kids rude to you when your mom left?" His gaze bores into Petal, and when I look up to her, I see tears in her eyes.

"They were. I was only a couple years older than you, but that doesn't stop kids from being jerks. I was picked on all through school 'cause my mom ran away with my sister." Shit, I didn't know that part either. I'm beginning to see her in a whole new light now. "It wasn't until I started modeling that anyone had anything nice to say to me, and it was never because they liked me. You just have to remember one thing, Mac."

"What's that?"

"Your mom leaving wasn't your fault. That's

completely on her. She's the one who is missing out on what great kids you and your sister are." I could kiss her again.

"You're leaving," Mac points out, and I want to kick my own ass again.

Petal's face saddens. "Also not your fault. This one is all on me."

"No, it's on Dad. 'Cause he's a hot head."

"Hey!" I glare down at my offspring, and the shit shrugs.

"No, sweetie, it's not. One day, you'll understand." Her voice is filled with her own sadness and frustration.

"Fuck," I mutter and scratch the back of my neck.

"You should just kiss her again, Dad, tell her she's ours now. Then I'd have a good mom." Mac's words don't just stun us; we're both speechless.

Petal laughs awkwardly before avoiding my gaze and hugging Mac. She whispers something in his ear that I don't hear and jogs off to her car. Not before I miss the lone tear tracking down her face as she does.

"Petal, wait!" She ignores me, hops in her car, and waves as she drives past us. Her despair is encompassing, and I know I have to do something or risk losing her forever.

"What did she say to you?"

Mac jumps in the truck, buckles his belt, and tells me, "That she would love to be our mom, but not if you don't love her." Slamming the door, he stares straight ahead.

"Fuck," I mutter again. I need to get this shit figured out and quick.

FIFTEEN

Cade

"**D**addy!" Lily squeals as I come downstairs. "You look so handsome." I stare down at myself and wonder what's wrong with how I usually dress.

"Shit, man, a tie?" Jace laughs.

"You're not going to dinner at the Queens, are you?" Beckett can barely get out between laughs.

"Shut the hell up, you two." I smack them both on the back of the head as I walk around the table to kiss Lily's cheek. "You keep these two in check, little girl. You're in charge."

"I will, Daddy! We're gonna play Princess!" Both men sober up quickly before they start their groaning.

"Oh, come on, prima, not again." Jace bangs his head on the table.

"Only if Jace wears the pink tiara this time," Beck grumbles as Mac hides behind a slice of pizza.

"But, Uncle Beck, you're pretty in pink." My girl pouts, and every man at the table caves to her desires with a mumbled fine.

Grabbing my wallet and keys, I head for the door. "I'll see you guys later." I'm out the door, second-guessing my casual tie as I straighten it above my leather vest and black tank. I'm not a fancy man. How I am now is about as dressy as I come. Combat boots and jeans are easier to ride my bike on, and it's too hot for a dress shirt.

Petal has no idea I'm coming over, that I fully intend on winning over her love tonight, or that I'm not taking no for an answer.

Cradling my Harley between my legs, I rev the engine as I back out of the driveway and head out to Huntington Beach. Traffic is backed up as usual, and I fight off my impatience by constantly checking my watch. The delay is driving me mad.

Finally, after an hour of driving, stopping, cursing, and weaving through stupid motorists, I'm outside her house. Her dad is on the porch with Roman, but Petal's car is nowhere in sight.

"She's not here, son," Wesley shouts.

Roman's tail thumps against the wooden deck as I approach. "I see that."

"Petal has put up with a lot of shit in her young life." I nod, knowing where this is about to go. "Never has she cried like she did today. I don't like seeing my baby cry."

"Neither do I, sir." I'd give anything to never see her cry.

"She loves you."

"I know." I was an idiot to not see it sooner.

"What are your intentions?"

I think about that for a minute because, while I love the woman, I don't know how to answer this in a way he'll appreciate. "Everything. I'm going to love her, marry her. I'm going to knock her up as often as I can, and I'm going to give her my heart, my kids, my life. There isn't a damn thing she won't have when I'm done with her."

"Don't mess with her, son," he warns and Roman growls. Damn dog's probably coming with her, too.

"Not in this lifetime."

"She's at Sunset Beach, near the Navy ship." With an appreciative nod, I jump on my bike and head down to her. Weaving through traffic and pushing the speed limits, I make it there in record time.

After parking my bike, I walk up onto the pathway and immediately see her standing in the water. She's wearing the same shorts and top as earlier. Jogging back down to my bike, I lock my wallet, keys, and phone in the saddle bag and run to her position. Kicking off my boots and socks, I wade into the water behind her, uncaring that my jeans are soaked up to my knees.

The water is warm, and she has no idea I'm on her until I wrap my arms around her chest, pulling her to my bulky frame.

Burying my face into her hair, I murmur, "I love you, Petal Davies. I've been a complete dick the past twenty-four hours, and I'll never be able to say sorry often enough."

When she spins to face me, instead of tears, I see a radiant smile on her face. "I heard your bike." Explains why she didn't jump when I touched her. "I'm mad at you, Cade. You hurt me yesterday."

"I didn't mean what I said, the way it sounded. I was more pissed because I hadn't laid claim to you and made it clear you were not only mine but our kids' as well. I was pissed because I knew you must have been confused and unsure of how to tell people you aren't Lily's mom without hurting her feelings. I was pissed because, from the day you walked into my office, late, a mess, and hot as fuck, I didn't do what I wanted to then."

"What's that?" She's breathless, and I know she knows exactly what I'm talking about.

"Kiss you." Leaning down, I scoop her up into my arms and lay a deep kiss on her mouth. I swallow her moans of pleasure, pressing for the gasps of desire I can feel rippling through both of us.

Walking blindly out of the ocean, I lay her down on the towel she has laid out and spread her legs, making room for myself. My hands roam every inch of flesh I can reach and, when they find the button of her shorts, I don't hesitate to undo them and slip a hand inside.

Touching her heat for the first time is like coming home. I need more of her. More of this, us. Together.

She fumbles with my belt buckle and whips it off, tossing it to the side before she works the zipper on my jeans down and my cock eagerly springs free. Her cool hands wrap around the monster, and I hiss from the chill.

"Fuck, that's cold," I mutter into her neck.

"I could warm you up." Her seductive proposition has me pulling back and gazing around us. Thankfully, we're on a pretty remote part of the beach, and there aren't any people around.

"I'll take you up on it." I groan as I pull away and she doesn't let go of my aching cock. "Jesus Christ, Petal." Pulling her shorts down her legs, I see the vines of her tattoo climb straight into her tiny purple panties, and I lean forward.

Running my nose along the crease of her covered folds, I nibble when I feel her shiver. "Cade, don't tease me." She groans and pushes up into my face.

"Never," I mumble. Pushing the material to the side, I waste no time in tasting her dewy lips. Flattening my tongue against her shaved pussy, I take long licks up her slit and swallow down every drop of desire she gives me.

"Cade," Petal snaps and pulls on my vest, bringing me up her body.

"Tell me," I groan, hating what I have to ask. "Are you a virgin?"

The vixen rolls her eyes. "No."

"Fuck." Anger and jealousy are a bitter bitch.

"Why?" Her voice is skeptical.

"I wanted to know if I had to be gentle. But now I'm pissed someone took my cherry," I hiss. My anger is unreasonable.

"Take me hard, Cade," she purrs in my ear as her thighs rub against my ribs. "Make this ache go away." Her words are like silk. "I can only do it myself so many times."

"Jesus, damn, Petal." It's a good thing I'm not standing because she just made me weak in the fucking knees.

SIXTEEN

Petal

From the first kiss to the I love you, I forgave Cade for his hurtful words. After explaining his anger away, I understand more, and it's nearly forgotten. From the moment we met, there's been immediate chemistry that we both fought to ignore. We denied what our hearts and bodies wanted, needed, and we paid the price.

I moan as I feel the heat of his cock against my core. I want him to take me. To own me. I want to own every part of him, too.

"Now, Cade," I demand. He's holding back and I don't like it. "Don't hold out on me now. Not after teasing me so well." I might have to hurt him if he does.

His head lifts, and his cocky grin is back. "I'd

never tease you, baby." I want to call him out on it, but he lines up his cock to my entrance and slams home to the hilt. I want to scream, but his hand covers my mouth as his balls slap against my ass. Cade lets out a deep groan as I flex my walls around his shaft and slowly lift my hips up to his body.

"Knock that shit off, woman." He still has a hand over my mouth, and his other grips my hip so roughly I know I'll have a bruise of his handprint.

Licking his palm, I close my eyes, tilt my head back, and continue to tease him until he gives me what I want. "Son of a bitch." He groans again and lets go of my mouth to hold my thigh. "Not one fucking sound from you, Petal, not one." His intense gaze bores into me with serious intent. I nod.

Before I can take a breath, his hips begin to move, and I'm lost completely in his clutches as he maneuvers inside of me. With each thrust of his hips, I can feel my pleasure building. It doesn't take long for my orgasm to rise and sweep me under a magical spell only he can weave.

"Mmm, Cade," I whine into his ear. His mouth kisses along my jaw, down to my neck where he sucks my rapidly beating pulse into his mouth until I know he's left his mark. "Again," I demand.

"Greedy little thing, aren't you?" His hot breath

in my ear has me biting my lip so I don't cry out. I can feel the sand under my exposed flesh as the towel shifts from his movements, but I can't bring myself to care.

"Come with me, Cade," I plea, digging my fingers into his back. My rapid heartbeat pounds between us, and I know I'm about to lose myself again. "Please, Cade."

"Whatever you want, babe." His thrusts come shorter and quicker as one of his hands works between our bodies, rubbing lightly on my clit, forcing my ecstasy to rush forth without warning.

"Ohhhh," I cry into his neck, biting down on his pulse and doing what he did to me as I feel him freeze and unload his cum into my body. The warmth as he groans out his pleasure has me melting back into his embrace.

As we lay satisfied, him still on top of me, his seed dripping slowly from my body, I can't help the words that slip free. "I love you, too, Cade."

"I want you to marry me." He hasn't lifted his head, so I don't know if he's serious, if it's spur of the moment, or even if he realizes what he said.

"You don't mean that." I try to laugh awkwardly and push him off me, but he doesn't budge.

"Baby, from the minute you shared those fucking

blueberries with Lily, I knew I was going to marry you. Love you. Give you my babies. You're it for me, Petal Davies, and nothing you say or do will change my mind." He says all of this while his head is still buried in my neck and his hips slowly start working me up again.

"But..." I lose my train of thought as Cade lifts my shirt and starts sucking a nipple into his mouth. I never knew I enjoyed that so much. My body buzzes and comes alive for him. Suddenly, I'm very agreeable. "Okay, Cade Larrabee, make an honest woman of me, but please, for the love of God, don't stop!"

"Not in this lifetime, soon to be wife of mine." His lips land on mine, and I don't know how it happens, but he fucks me through three orgasms of my own and one of his without breaking the kiss or us getting caught.

He mentioned babies. If there isn't one coming in nine months now, I'll be shocked.

SEVENTEEN

Cade

S tumbling through the front door of the house,
I know the kids are with Beckett at his place
for the night, so when I toss Petal's shirt off, I'm
shocked to hear "Watch it!" in the sound of Jace's
voice.

A very naked Petal ignores it—or doesn't hear
him—and drops to her knees in front of me, unzip-
ping my pants and attacking my hard dick like a
fucking lollipop.

"Holy shit!" Jace whispers, fascinated by the
naked woman on the floor in front of me.

"Get the fuck out!" I shout at him, barely able to
hold myself together as this woman pulls me apart.
Staring down at her, I see a wicked gleam in her eye
as she swallows deeply around the head of my dick,

and I swear I go blind for a minute. "Now, Jace," I hiss at my friend. Petal's eyes widen but she doesn't stop.

"I'm going, I'm going, but fuck, she's got one nice ass," Jace mutters as he slowly walks to the front door and, I swear to God, if she wasn't swallowing like my dick is her lifeline, I'd kick his ass. "Sure you don't wanna share?" I know he's kidding, but his tone says otherwise. He wants her, and I don't fucking blame him, but she's mine.

"Find your own woman, Jace, and get the fuck out of my house before I kill you." I groan when I feel Petal's fingers tickling my sack, and all I want to do is unload down her throat. Watch as she swallows down every last drop.

Jace shakes his head and closes the door behind him. As soon as he's gone, I pull out of Petal's mouth, needing a deeper connection. Her whine doesn't stop me. "Turn around." I growl the words like the beast I'm feeling like. As soon as her ass is facing me, I spread her cheeks and work my dick against both holes. Dipping the tip into her tight little pussy, I push until I'm balls deep and can feel myself against her completely.

"So deep," she whimpers, cocking her ass up at

me closer so I go further. "Ohhhhh, Cade." Her soft voice makes my dick twitch.

Draping my body over hers, I grip her hair in a tight knot. "You ever had it in the ass, Petal?" I'd fucking kill to be her first there. And her last.

"No." Her back arches and she wiggles against me.

"Good," I growl into her ear as I sit back up. Pushing her down further, I instruct her, "Gimme your hands." Reaching back, her body is vibrating with anticipation. Placing a hand on each cheek, I help her spread them apart, exposing her little rosebud just begging for my dick. "Don't move." I thrust inside her pussy a few more times to get her nicely worked up before I slowly drag my dick out and begin playing with her ass.

I can see her nails digging into her cheeks, the way she's tensing and then forcing herself to relax as I push on the small ring of muscles trying to keep the head of my dick out. Her pussy juice makes for the perfect lube as I forge my way inside her forbidden hole.

"Christ. Yeah." My words are nearly incoherent as I admire the way her body accepts me. I'm only three inches in, and she's writhing beneath me and barely able to control her moans of desire. "Do you like it, Petal?"

She's quiet for a minute before answering me. "Yes." This time, it's her pushing back onto me and, before either of us realizes it, I'm in her ass to my balls and my eyes cross.

"Fuck," I hiss. Gripping her wrists in my hands, I hold on to her. Using her arms as leverage, I push and pull her on my dick.

"Oh, God!" she screams, and her upper body flushes red as she comes for me again. "Cade!" Her scream will likely wake the neighbors, but all I want to do is make her scream louder.

"Petal, so fucking tight," I groan, letting go of her arms, and they flop to the floor. Her entire body relaxes as I grip her hips, holding her up as I thrust wildly out of control. My dick thickens and my balls draw up to my body. Right as I'm about to come, I pull out just enough that I can watch my cum squirt onto her body.

"Oh my God," she whispers as I rub it into her flesh, covering her in my essence as my body depletes itself. "Cade, that was..."

I wait for her to continue, but she's breathless.

"Hot? So fucking hot," I answer for her.

"Erotic," she murmurs. "Can we do it again?" Her

body drops to the ground, my cum drying on her ass and lower back as she looks up at me hopefully.

"Shower first, then I'm back in that sweet little pussy of yours," I tell her, and she rolls onto her back, spreading her legs wide open.

With a single digit, she rubs lightly on her clit and pouts. "You mean this empty pussy that needs your tongue, right now?"

"Fucking hell, woman," is all I can say as I lean forward and wrap my lips around her clit, sucking and biting the little piece of flesh until her hands are trying to pull me away and she's screaming her pleasure again.

"Cade, it hurts," she cries out but still pushes her hips up into my mouth. "Harder!" Her wish is my command. Lifting her hips higher, I don't let up as one orgasm rolls into another and she's trying to push me off with her feet on my shoulders.

Finally giving her relief, I grin. "You asked for it, baby."

"I know." She's breathless as I pull her to her feet, her juices dripping down my chin as I pull her in for a kiss. "Mmm, who knew I tasted like blueberries?" Her laughter is light as I carry her up to the bathroom, cleaning up and a bed my only destination for the next twelve hours at least.

EIGHTEEN

Petal

Lying in Cade's bed, his light snoring in my ear and hand on my stomach, I stare up at the ceiling of his room. Sunlight is just peaking in from the window. I know I should be getting up and doing something, but for the first time in my life, I feel like I'm right where I'm supposed to be.

I'm not worried about the shift in our relationship or how his kids will take it; I know that Cade and I are right. We belong together.

The problem is, I can't help this niggling feeling in the back of my mind that something is off. I had this feeling the day my dad had his heart attack, and no matter how hard I try, I can't shake it off.

As I slip free of the bed, Cade rolls onto his back and the sheet slides down to his hips. I take a moment to admire his sexy physique. His tattoos are dark and more tribal than anything else as far as I've been able to tell, and his muscles just won't quit. The defined abs and that perfect V leading down to the promised land make me as dumb as any girl.

I'm still amazed he wants me, and I get to call him mine. After spending most of the night making love, I'm a little sore today but I wouldn't change it for the world.

Quietly grabbing a folded t-shirt from the chair in the corner, I sneak out of his room and head downstairs. The benefit of being his kids' nanny for a month is that I know where everything is in the house. I don't have to be nosy while searching for coffee, and I know just what Cade likes for breakfast.

Filling the water reservoir for coffee, I scoop out the grounds from the container to what Cade likes—dark and strong—and hit the on button. It only takes seconds for the scent to fill the kitchen as I put bacon on a pan and stick it in the oven.

Deciding to whip up a batch of waffles, I grab the waffle maker I found about a week ago shoved in the back of the pantry and plug it in, spraying oil on both sides of the griddle. The silence of the house isn't something I'm used to as I work, so I snatch

Cade's phone off the counter and search out his music, already knowing it's not my normal style.

Some rock tune slices through the air, and I find I don't mind it too much. Swaying my hips, I dance around the kitchen as I grab plates and utensils, setting the table. Waffles and bacon done, I pour our coffee and bring everything over to the table. Spinning as I dance, I see Cade standing in the doorway watching me, a smile on his face and lust in his stare. The hard-on he's sporting isn't even close to being hidden by his basketball shorts either.

"Good morning." I don't have to move closer to him because he comes to me. Without a word, his lips are on mine and he's lifting me up onto the counter so I'm the perfect height for his erection to press into my bare heat.

From the look on his face as he pulls away, he knows I'm not wearing anything either. Still not speaking, he pushes his shorts down and slowly enters my body. All it takes is a small touch for my body to ignite for him.

"I had a dream about you." He groans in my ear as he slowly slides in and out of my core.

"Oh, yeah?" I'm breathless.

"It ended with my ring on your finger and my

baby in your belly." I'm starting to think he's obsessed with this idea.

"It did?" I can play innocent.

"I'd like to work on that." He captures my lips again, and my heart nearly bursts from my chest as his tongue mimics his cock in movement.

"I think you have." I whisper when I have to pull back to catch my breath. "I made waffles."

"I saw that."

"And bacon."

"Uh-huh." His eyes are closed as if he's pained.

"Coffee, too." I'm panting now and feel my release coming.

"Petal." My name sounds like a prayer on his lips as I feel his warmth let go inside of me, and I follow him over the edge into bliss.

"Good morning," he mutters against my lips, kissing me lightly as he helps me down from the counter.

I can feel his seed dripping down my thighs, and I don't mind one bit. "Indeed, it is." I'm sure I have a goofy grin on my face as we sit down to eat.

NINETEEN

Cade

"I was an ass, man. I need to make it up to her." I look at my best friend who shakes his head at me.

"I'd say she's forgiven you, bro." Jace doesn't get it.

"Maybe, but I haven't." I hate how cold my words were to her after Lily's recital. There isn't enough in this world I could do to make it up to Petal to say I'm sorry. I know she's forgiven me, she told me so, but I want to do more for her.

"Hasn't Beckett taken the kids to your parents' for the weekend?" They left early this morning and have already arrived. I'd bet Beck is on his way back now. My brother is quiet, but lately, he's been more so. I'm starting to become worried about him.

"Yeah, I wanted some alone time with Petal

because those runts take up all her free time." They're already planning all the things they want to do with her, and Lily has even asked if she can start calling her Mom. In their minds, it's already a done deal. Petal is ours, and there's nothing that is going to change that.

"So, take her on a date. Go to Santa Monica, be silly tourists. I bet she's into that kind of thing." I'm honestly shocked Jace isn't harassing me about how we stumbled in last night and what he watched Petal doing to me. I figured I'd have to kick his ass today.

"Is it too soon to get married?" I force a laugh because I'm not really kidding. The sooner I can tie her to me, the better. She's off running errands for Lily and Mac today. School is finished next week, and she wanted to make sure they had new clothes for the summer and some arts and crafts so they aren't bored. I think she mentioned something about summer camp, too, but I was too busy watching her wash herself in the shower.

"I'd think so, yeah. Both your folks might be pissed to miss it." Shit.

"I want her tied to me. The sooner the better." Jace shakes his head again and mumbles something about me being hopeless as he walks out of my office into the back of the shop. We have a customer coming in today to discuss a custom bike she wants for her future husband. She's supposed to be here any minute now.

Going through payroll paperwork, invoices and expenditures, I'm not sure if my accountant is going to hate me or love me this quarter. I finally listened to him and downloaded the software he's been begging me to use for a couple of years now. It's supposed to make doing this easier for both of us. After spending a few hours this week alone inputting expenses, I'm inclined to agree with him. I just won't admit it.

The bell above the door jingles, and I look up at the clock to see this woman is an hour late. I might turn her business away on principal alone. I don't have time for people who can't appreciate my time.

"Ms. Hendrix," I stand up to greet her, "in the future, please be mindful of our appointment times." Standing in the doorway, I see it's not some almost newlywed wanting to get her future husband a present. "Son of a bitch, Steph, what the hell are you doing here?"

"Hello, Cade." Her seductive voice isn't as sexy as I once found it, and my dick definitely doesn't twitch anymore.

"Get out." I won't have this bitch hurting Petal because she's here.

"But, Cade." Her husky voice only serves to piss me off. "You know you want me back."

Shaking my head, I chuckle because it's either that or lose my temper. "No, Steph, I want nothing to do with you. Leave." Turning my back on her reddening face, I hope that's the end of it.

I should have known better.

"Cade Larrabee!" I hear her heels clicking behind me, and when I turn around, she drops her coat to reveal her nude body, jumps in my arms, and plants her lips on mine.

Before I get a chance to react, I hear the fucking bell ringing again, and the crackle of anger lighting up the room is like lightning striking as Petal storms over to us.

I'm not sure what to expect, but when she grips a fistful of Stephanie's hair and yanks the woman's head back, the shock on my ex's face is nearly comical. "Take your slutty hands off of my man before I remove them from your body."

Damn. My girl's got bite.

"You're assaulting me!" Stephanie screeches, and Jace comes running into the front.

"Not yet, I'm not. But I promise I will if you ever

come back." Petal stands tall, not a worried bone in her body.

"You bitch!" Stephanie spins around, hand raised, poised to slap Petal, but Roman's fierce growl and displayed teeth stop her in her tracks. "Ahhhh!" She screams and tries to hide behind me.

"Get. Out." Petal grits between clenched teeth.

Rushing around Petal and Roman, Steph grabs her coat, slips it on, and opens the door. "I'll have you arrested," she calls as she leaves, and Petal ignores her to glare at me.

"I didn't invite her." I raise my hands.

"You have bad taste in women," Petal mutters and pushes past me into my office.

"Well, I did. But I choose you, so it's not all bad." When I go to wrap my arms around her waist, she pushes me back.

"First, your kids chose me, then I chose you. You were slow. Second, clean clothes and brush your teeth first. I want no part of that walking disease touching me." Dropping my credit card on the desk, she finally turns to me, an unexpected smile on her. "You have to love my dog now." Cocking her hip, her attitude surprises me. There's no jealousy or anger.

"You're not mad?" I sure as hell hope this isn't

one of those times where she fakes being fine when she's stewing inside.

"About droopy tits?" Her laughter is genuine. "Not even close. She's a whore I spotted a mile away. I know I don't have to worry about you. You proved quite thoroughly how much you love me."

"Thank fuck." I walk toward her, but she puts her hand up to stop me.

"Not kidding, shower first. Besides, if I didn't trust you, or I thought you were straying, I'd let Roman eat your manly bits." The fucking dog licks his chops like he has any idea what we're talking about.

"You wouldn't." I glare at the mutt.

"Try me." Petal winks and walks back out of my office.

Like the lovesick dog on her heels, I follow. I'd follow this woman to the ends of the earth and back if she let me. I lucked the fuck out when she came into my life, and there is nothing that will make me screw that up.

TWENTY

Petal

ONE MONTH LATER.

"Stop fidgeting," Cade demands, placing his hands over the top of mine. His parents are meeting us for a family dinner. Cade insisted on taking everyone out because he didn't want me stressing over the food while meeting his parents for the first time.

I've spoken to his mother, Gina, weekly since the kids came home, and we get along great. But a face to face is always so much more intimate.

After our last fiasco with Stephanie, where Roman scared the daylights out her, she hasn't been back either. Things have been wonderful between Cade, the kids, and I, and I'm terrified this is where things will go bad. That his parents won't like me.

"I can't help it," I snap back at him. Lily and Mac

are busy entertaining my dad with stories of our trip to the beach this week when Roman ran away from a crab. Yeah, my big ass dog was afraid of a crustacean. It was kind of hilarious.

"Here they are," Cade whispers in my ear, kissing my neck and making shivers race down my spine.

"Oh my goodness! It is her!" My heart sinks by the unclear meaning of Gina's words.

"I don't understand…" I look at Matt for clarification, but he rolls his eyes and introduces himself to my father.

"You're the young lady who did those makeup commercials all those years ago." Well, crap.

"Umm, well, probably. But I haven't done those in well over six years." I hope this doesn't mean she hates me.

Swiping her hand through the air, Gina talks right over my nerves. "Of course, you haven't. That's such a tough industry, so much pressure."

"It's why I left. I never was one to follow blindly." I smile, feeling myself relax as we get into a conversation about my modeling, what I think of the industry as a whole, and how the tides are finally changing where the girls get to have an opinion rather than be mindless zombies.

The evening progresses so quickly, I'm sad when

it's time to say goodnight. As I'm walking my dad to his car, I see Gina and Matt handing something to Cade before grabbing the kids and rushing off with them. They're leaving Cade and me alone for the first night since we got together.

"So, now what?" I look up at him. All I get is his signature cocky grin as he grabs my hand and walks us toward the pier off the beach.

Cade is silent as he leads me onto the walkway, hand in hand. I watch him for any clue of what's going on. While nervous about his silence, I'm not worried. This man tells me how much he loves me on a daily basis. With him, I know I never have to worry about where I stand.

"You're very quiet," I point out in the hopes he'll say something. All he told me we were doing tonight was dinner with our parents.

The sound of waves as they hit the shore is soothing when he pulls me to a stop. "I know you didn't have it easy growing up. With your mom taking your sister and leaving, then having to work and worry about school, I know Wes worried about you a lot."

"Okay." All things I knew.

"Tonight wasn't just about our families meeting, Petal." Turning to face me fully, Cade shows me a sweeter side he likes to hide from the world. Leaning forward to kiss me on the cheek, he pulls a box from his pocket and gets down on one knee.

"Oh, God." Tears well, and I bite my lip to keep my emotions in check. He's said a bunch of times he wants us to get married, but he's never done anything to make it official. Now, I know why.

"I thought hiring a nanny would only help me keep my kids happy, give them more than what I could. I didn't expect that hiring you would bring me this compulsive desire to own another human being completely to myself. I wanted to do this sooner, but my mother begged me to use my grandmother's ring. She said it was good luck. I love you, Petal Davies, and I can't wait for you to be my wife." Slipping the simple rose gold ring on my finger, he stands and scoops me up into his arms.

Not even asking. The cocky shit.

Tangling my tongue with his, I bite on his lip and pull back. "What would you have done if I said no?"

"Why do you think I didn't ask you?" Smartass.

"You're lucky I love you, Cade Larrabee."

Who knew I'd find an everlasting love for taking care of kids?

Epilogue One

CADE

One Year Later.

"Don't freak out." Petal walks into my office, her small baby bump leading the way, with a singing Lily behind her.

"What the hell?" Lily is leading a small puppy by the leash behind her, and Roman is hot on their heels. "Why does our daughter have a puppy?" When I say puppy, I use the word loosely, because this thing is a beast.

"Well, we were at the pet store. Roman needed some things, and there was a new litter of puppies, and, uh, well..." My wife shrugs. My lovely, beautiful, mother of my children, the other half of my soul, has a compulsion issue. She can't say no to these kids about anything.

"We have a baby coming," I point out as she walks around my desk to sit in my lap.

"And he's going to be so handsome, just like his daddy and big brother." Her lips start a slow climb up my neck and across my jaw.

"Eeewww," Lily groans and leaves the office. Roman and the puppy follow behind her.

"Gross, guys, get a room." Mac rolls his eyes as he pops his head in.

"Shut the door and we'll have one," I bark at the boy.

It slams behind them, and Lily's singing gets louder. "You're pushing it lately, woman." I slap her thigh lightly, making her jump in my lap.

Turning so she's facing me with her legs on either side of my hips, I'm not lost on the skirt she's wearing. This woman will do anything she can to tease me.

"I know, but I can't help it." Her sneaky hands slip down my chest and begins unbuckling my belt before going for the button and zipper of my jeans.

Reaching under her skirt, I'm both pissed and turned on that she's not wearing anything. "What the fuck, Petal?"

"You like it." Her aloof shrug tips me over, and I plant her fine ass on the edge of my desk as I stand.

"Doesn't mean you should be risking it, especially in public for fuck's sake." I sound madder than I actually am.

"I didn't, I took them off in the bathroom when we got here." Her devilish grin is my last straw. Flipping her skirt up, I'm greeted with her naked cunt waiting for me to fill her up.

When I slide my dick across her folds, she sighs and drops her thighs farther open for me. Her breathy sounds never cease to make me hornier in the moments before I enter her body.

"Oh, Cade." She sighs. Being pregnant has calmed some of her brazen attitude, but she's still open about what she wants. And she never hesitates to tell me anything. "Long, slow strokes." She bats her lashes at me, and I narrow my gaze on her.

"You like to tease me, don't you?" I thrust in and out, excruciatingly slowly as she raises up on her elbows.

"I enjoy the build-up. I like the pain when you take me to another universe, and I certainly desire seeing you let loose from the slow burn."

"Fuck, I love you." Snaking my hand behind her neck, I bring her closer to capture her mouth in a deep kiss, exploring every crevice and swallowing her moans as I feel her walls shudder around me.

"I love you back, dear husband."

If there's nothing else I did right in my life, falling in love with Petal was the one thing I've perfected. She's always going to be the girl worth fighting for, for me.

Epilogue Two

PETAL

Six Months Later.

"Merry Christmas!" I'm always the first one awake on Christmas morning. It used to drive my dad nuts how much I loved the holiday. But now, with Mac, Lily, and our new little boy, Wheeler, I love it a little bit more.

"Mommy!" Lily jumps from the bed and runs to grab my hand as we wake up the rest of the house. Cade's parents are here as well as my dad. Beckett and Jace are sleeping down in the living room. They'll get a rude awakening any minute now.

As I check in on Wheeler—he was up a couple of hours ago for a feeding and I'm hoping he sleeps through the chaos that will be our morning—the doorbell rings.

"Who the fuck is that?" I hear grumbled from downstairs. Lily dances at the bottom of the stairs, waiting on Cade and me to come down.

I see Jace answer the door, and it isn't until Lily's next words that I even wonder who it is. "You look just like my mommy." Mac and Lily never hesitated to call me Mom, even before the adoption paperwork went through a few months ago. For all intents and purposes, they're my children.

"Jace?" I call as Cade comes up behind me. If Lily is saying that, I have a feeling I know who it is, but I don't know how to process it.

"I've got you, babe. Just breathe." After we got married, a short month after he didn't propose, Cade sent a private investigator out to find not only Candace so she could sign away whatever rights she might have had, but to find my mom and Calla, too. It's been a year and a half, and I never thought it would happen. Let alone today of all days.

"Hey, uh, Petal, you got a sister?" Jace looks just as stunned as me and, because I know him so well, I know he's been smacked in the head by desire.

"Calla?" I whisper as I see her for the first time in more than a decade.

"Petal?" Her eyes fill with tears as she rushes toward me. Her arms wrap around my waist, and I feel hot tears track down my cheeks.

"How... what... how?" I'm speechless. I don't know what to say.

"I asked him not to tell you yet. I'm so sorry." My little sister's words are rushed and jumbled.

"What are you talking about?" I push her back by the shoulders as everyone in the house watches us. Except for my dad. He sleeps like the dead. Probably didn't even hear me and Lily come into his room.

"Lil, go get Grandpa please," I ask. I know he'll do anything for her.

I hold Calla in my arms for so long; I never thought I'd see her again. "Come, girls, let's sit." Gina ushers us to the table.

It's only a few minutes before I hear Lily and Dad coming down the stairs, and we stand up together. I grip her hand in mine and pray this goes over well.

Dad stops in his tracks, Lily in his arms, and stares. "Calla?" His voice cracks and tears fill his eyes, the same as ours.

"Daddy." I'm surprised she remembers him. She was so young when Momma ran away with her.

Without putting Lily down, Dad walks over and

159

pulls Calla into his hold while Cade wraps an arm around me. "You doing okay?" he whispers in my ear.

"Yeah, Cade, I really am." Even though I have a ton of question about what happened and where they've been, I know this is a miracle I never thought would happen.

I have my family. The one I created and the one I was born into. I don't think this Christmas could get any better.

The End!

Thank you for reading A Girl Worth Fighting For. The next book in the series is <u>The Girl Who was Meant to be Mine</u> .
Listen to the Spotify playlist now.
Be sure to check out the rest of the Uncontrolled Heroes series too.
Please consider signing up for <u>KL's Confessions</u> for first chance at cover reveals, new release info, ARCs, contests and more.

What to read next?

If you enjoyed A Girl Worth Fighting For, then I think you'll really like <u>The Girl Who was Meant to be Mine</u>.
Get hooked by reading the excerpt below!

Jace

For six months now, I've been frequenting the diner across the street from Controlled Bikes after bribing the owner to give me Calla's schedule. I don't believe she suspects anything. I've been coming here long before she showed up, just not nearly as often.

From the minute I opened that door on Christmas morning, I've damn near been in love with her. Something inside me shifted when her nervous gaze met mine. I intimidate her, though. Every time we're in the same room together, she damn near hides behind Petal.

I think we've said maybe two dozen sentences to each other because she's alarmed by my size. If I wasn't comfortable in my own skin, I'd be insulted. But given the fact, she's a good foot shorter than me and weighs probably a hundred pounds soaking wet, I'm not surprised. People who don't know me get a little freaked out. The muscles and tattoos don't help.

I've never given a shit about any of it before either. But with Calla, I try to remain low-key and unobtrusive because I want her trust. I want her to look at me with something else other than fear. I get the feeling that's the only emotion she's truly familiar with, unfortunately.

Petal tries so hard to get Calla over to the house quite a bit, but the younger woman declines as politely and often as she can. Petal won't say anything because she doesn't want to push her sister away, but Cade and I are about fed up.

Cade, his brother Beckett, and I grew up together. We've run around our entire lives. Own a business together. I've never felt like anything other than the third brother in our trio. We're close. When one of us hurts, we all do. And Petal is hurting. Lily and Mac are dying to know their aunt better, but the baby doesn't care too much beyond the kids, Petal, and Cade.

Lily turns five this weekend, though, and I'm here to guilt Calla into coming to the party. Petal has been stressing about asking her because she doesn't want to be let down again, and I intend to make sure that doesn't happen.

Acknowledgments

A great big huge massive thanks to my girl Mayra Statham for inviting me to be a part of this project. Seriously, thank her for Cade & Petal's story, because otherwise, I never would have written it.

About the Author

KL Donn is a USA Today Bestselling Author of dark contemporary romance, a genre she has made her own with series such as the Adair Empire/Legacy, Mafia Made, Kings of the Underworld and more. As a Canadian author Krystal plans to write a brand-new series called Hello! Summer, based in the beautiful Rocky Mountains of her home province, Alberta.

Unafraid of a new challenge, Krystal loves bringing you stories that will break your heart and heal it all in one breath. With over 70 published titles since 2015, she has many more books planned for the future and intends on continuing with some next generation spin-offs for current series as well as brand new characters in new series such as, Kings of the Underworld, The Good & The Bad Things, and Bad Men Possessing Good Girls.

On her off time, she's bingeing Supernatural, Grey's Anatomy, raising 4 amazing children, and carting children from Soccer, Football, and Ball

Hockey 6 days a week. Married for more than half her life, she experienced her own happily ever after with husband Steve, at just 17. You'll find them both at book signings once or twice a year, she's the shy one, he's there to tell you all about the books his wife writes and how proud he is of her.

Krystal loves connecting with readers so please feel free to get in touch with her at any of the platforms below:

KL's Deviant Readers | Facebook | Instagram

Or follow her releases on:

BookBub | Goodreads | Newsletter

Also by KL Donn

Kings of the Underworld

<u>Obsess</u> | Protector | Obey | Predator | Monster | Power | Own | Primal | Purity | Outlier | Prey

Adair Legacy

<u>Broken Princess</u> | <u>Tortured Duchess</u> | <u>Killer Prince</u> | <u>Delicate Dame</u> | <u>Dark Knight</u>

Adair Empire

<u>King</u> | <u>Luther</u> | <u>Castiel</u> | <u>Atticus</u> | <u>Carver</u> | <u>Trinity</u>

The Odessa Organization

<u>Anton</u> | <u>Vasyl</u> | <u>Petro</u> | <u>Forgive My Sins</u> | <u>The Sweetest Agony</u>

Damaged Love Series

<u>Unraveling Love</u> | <u>Broken Love</u> | Fractured Love | Tarnished Love

Decker Brothers Duet

<u>Wanted</u> | <u>Time Bomb</u>

The Throwaways

Cage & Magnolia | Dorian & Clementine

Mafia Made

His Kingdom | His Jailbird | His Fight | His Solace | His Protection | His Wicked Obsession

Task Force 779

Missing in Action | Explosive Encounter | Nowhere To Run | Dangerous Affair

Neighbor Novels

Possessive Neighbor | Reclusive Neighbor | Innocent Neighbor

Power of Vashchenko

Taking Emmaline | Protecting Scarlett | Claiming Madelyn

Uncontrolled Heroes

A Girl Worth Fighting For | The Girl Who was Meant to be Mine | Loving the Girl in the Tutu

Daniels Family

Until Arsen | With Kol | Embers Falling | Before Noah | Dreaming of California

Those Malcolm Boys

Obsessive Addiction | Accidental Obsession | Arrogantly Obsessed

Timeless Love

Once Upon A Time | Happily Ever After

In His Arms Series

Safe, In His Arms | Bullied, In His Arms | Coached, In His Arms

Naughty Tales

Dirty | Treat Me | Snowed In | Cuffed

Love Letters

Dear Killian | Dear Gage | Dear Maverick | Dear Desmond | Dear Lena | Dear Steele

Stand Alone Books

Holding Out For A Hero | Love Comes After | Saving Their Princess | London's Calling | Holly's Knight | Last Chance Love | Dear, Soldier of Mine | Little Girl | Room Twenty-Eight | Untouchable

Books in KU | Free Books | Boxsets

Audio Books

Are you a listener rather than a reader?
Check out these Audio books now, with more
coming soon!

<u>Wanted</u>

<u>Time Bomb</u>

<u>Unraveling Love</u>

<u>Holding Out For A Hero</u>

Tell Me More...

Am I missing books? So glad you asked! Yes, there are three series missing from my list of other works. The Protectors Series, The Possessed Series, & The Hogan Brothers. Why? Extra glad you asked again!

Because I will be rewriting all 3 series and making significant changes to them. Like what? Great question! These are my only series that are written in 3rd person point of view. While I love writing in 3rd and 1st POV, I feel like now is the time to make the changes and do a ton of rewriting on all 3 series. December 31st, 2023 will be the last day you'll be able to purchase these series until they come back.

What's going to change in them? Aside from going from 3rd to 1st person POV, I'll be doing a complete rewrite, keeping key elements and story-lines, but there will be tons of changes, including new titles, new series name, new covers, and anything else I can think of. While I hope to begin re-releasing them once again in mid-late 2025, I'm not giving any dates just yet, which is why you should totally signup for my newsletter to get all the details in the future.

Once the re-writing process has been finished, I'll be looking for beta readers to make sure these books come back better than ever, so there's more incentive to join my newsletter too! KL's Confessions – Newsletter

Printed in Great Britain
by Amazon